TRUST AND TREACHERY

"You have no choice," Adam said, but the part of Amanda's mind that still could think knew that if she resisted him he would let her go. She put up a hand to push him away and felt his lips move from her mouth to the hollow of her throat. And the protesting hand she had raised buried itself, caressingly, in his crisp, black hair.

Afterward, as they lay together, she said, "What are we going to do?"

"Trust me," he said. "I would cut out my heart before I hurt you."

She laughed shakenly. "I don't care if you hurt me. Just so long as you love me."

Amanda had entered a shadowy world of betrayal, where a nation's secrets were stolen with the same skill as a woman's heart—and where the man who asked her to trust him was master of every trick of the traitor's art. . . .

A KIND OF HONOR

More Delightful Regency Romances from SIGNET

A KIND OF
—HONOR—
by Joan Wolf

He hath a kind of honor sets him off
More than a mortal seeming.
—*Cymbeline*, I, vi

A SIGNET BOOK
NEW AMERICAN LIBRARY

NAL BOOKS ARE AVAILABLE AT QUANTITY DISCOUNTS WHEN USED TO PROMOTE PRODUCTS OR SERVICES. FOR INFORMATION PLEASE WRITE TO PREMIUM MARKETING DIVISION, NEW AMERICAN LIBRARY, 1633 BROADWAY, NEW YORK, NEW YORK 10019.

SIGNET TRADEMARK REG. U.S. PAT. OFF. AND FOREIGN COUNTRIES REGISTERED TRADEMARK—MARCA REGISTRADA HECHO EN CHICAGO, U.S.A.

SIGNET, SIGNET CLASSIC, MENTOR, PLUME, MERIDIAN, AND NAL Books are published by New American Library, 1633 Broadway, New York, New York 10019

First Printing, July, 1980

2 3 4 5 6 7 8 9 10

PRINTED IN THE UNITED STATES OF AMERICA

Prologue

Burgos, Spain, October 1812

It was raining when Major Lord Stanford reached Burgos to find the English army's siege not progressing well at all. The scene was dreary: Lord Wellington's army was camped around the outworks of the castle, lodged uncomfortably in open huts made of branches that did very little to protect them from the rain and the cold, both of which were unusually severe for a Spanish autumn. Above them, perched on its eyrie of rock, stood Burgos Castle, seemingly impregnable. The siege had been in progress for almost a month, and so far only the outworks had been captured.

Stanford found the army's commander in a gloomy frame of mind, but his face lightened perceptibly upon seeing the dark face of Adam Todd. The young man, Wellington's chief intelligence officer, reported with a lucid and passionless economy. When he had concluded, Wellington's face was even clearer. "Well, that is good news, at any rate," he remarked briskly. "That means I can go ahead with my plans for the spring." Wellington was often accused of not trusting his subordinates, but he seemed perfectly willing to rely on Lord Stanford's information. "Stanford is invaluable to me," he once was heard to say, "because he is always accurate."

Wellington's face looked more hawklike than ever

when Stanford asked, "How are things progressing here, sir?"

"They aren't," Wellington snapped. "I have five engineer officers and eight men. As usual we are lacking vital personnel. I don't even have proper siege guns: three long eighteen-pounders and a few howitzers are all we have. And we are short of ammunition."

Stanford thought of the sheer heights of Burgos Castle. "Good God, sir," he said.

"Good God indeed," returned Lord Wellington. "The truth is, Stanford, that, equipped as we are, the British army is not capable of carrying on a regular siege."

The commander's gloom had spread to the rest of the army, as Stanford discovered during the next few days. Line regiments were scarcely ever any good as amateur engineers, and the First Division, which was at Burgos, had no experience in siegework at all. The men hated it; Wellington was even forced to upbraid the officers for their lack of enthusiasm.

The French inside the castle, led by a brilliant commander, showed every sign of holding out forever. The English lacked the artillery for a knockout blow, and assaults on the wall were piecemeal rather than smashing. Wellington did not want to incur again the heavy losses which he had sustained at the successful siege of Badajoz.

Stanford found the whole spectacle appallingly depressing and, out of sheer frustration, led one of the assaults himself on October 14. Stanford's combat role in the war so far had been limited; his duties were intelligence and reconnaissance. But the need at Burgos was for field officers, so Stanford took a platoon of men and for the first time a mine was successfully sprung and two breeches in the outer defense carried.

Their minor success did not last long. Three days later the French swept down on the trenches, where Stanford was once again lending the encouragement of his presence. Stanford managed to evacuate most of the workmen and the tools, but he was shot twice, in the leg and the hip, and by the time his men carried him to safety he had lost quite a lot of blood.

The loss of Stanford seemed to knock the heart out of Wellington. He ordered a last assault on October 18, which was successfully repulsed by the defenders. Then he ordered the siege lifted and the army slipped out of Burgos after dark on October 21. The wounded were sent before them in spring carts, their wheels muffled with straw.

They reached Salamanca on November 8, and Dr. McGrigor attended to the wounded. Then began the retreat to winter quarters at Ciudad Rodrigo. It rained in torrents. The men marched knee-deep in mud, waded through streams swollen into rivers, and went without food for four days, as the commissary stores had mistakenly been sent ahead. Stanford was only intermittently conscious in the jolting wagon, his awareness dulled by fever and pain. Finally, the army reached Ciudad Rodrigo, where Dr. McGrigor gave special attention to Viscount Stanford. Transport was arranged to send the severely wounded on to Oporto, where they would be placed on a ship for England.

Wellington came to see Stanford before the wagons left. He stood for a long moment looking down at the still face on the pallet, the black hair in stark contrast to the pallor even a tan could not disguise. He put his hand on Stanford's arm. A moment later the black lashes lifted, revealing heavy blue eyes. "I expect to see you back in a few months, Stanford," he said authoritatively, and a shadowy smile passed across the white face below him.

As he walked away from the wagons Wellington's look of sheer despair prevented anyone from talking to him. Suddenly he turned to Pakenham, who was beside him. "He was worth a brigade to me," he said. And walked away.

Chapter 1

I do not think
So fair an outward and such stuff within
Endows a man but he. ·
—Cymbeline, I, i, 22–25

There was a traitor at the Horse Guards. That was the conclusion come to by Lord Bathurst, the war minister, and the military secretary, Lord Menteith. It was not a conclusion they were at all happy to reach, but in the light of the evidence it was indisputable. For the last six months information had been leaking to Paris at an alarming rate—information of a highly confidential nature. At this point in time, with Wellington's new offensive planned for the spring, it was essential to maintain secrecy.

"Damme, we can have Boney finished off in a year's time if all goes according to plan," Lord Bathurst had said. "According to Wilson, he lost half a million men in Russia. The Swedes are talking to us now. Prussia and Austria are wavering. If Wellington has a decisive victory in Spain it could well be the push they need to abandon Bonaparte and join with us." Bathurst had slammed his hand down on the desk. "We must find out who is sending that information! I leave it to you, Menteith."

So now Lord Menteith sat at his desk at the Horse Guards, worry clouding his pleasant brown eyes. He was a stocky, medium-sized man of about forty whose brown hair as yet showed no trace of gray. He was intelligent, capable, and utterly reliable, which is why he was in his present position. But he was damned if he knew how to go about unearthing a traitor. It frightened and humiliated him to think that one of the men he knew and trusted could be in fact an enemy agent.

He looked once again at the papers on his desk and opened for the fourth time the file that lay on top. It contained the records of Adam Todd, Viscount Stanford, lately invalided home from Spain. He had no idea if Stanford was recovered enough to come to London, but if he could Menteith thought he might be just the man he needed. Lord Wellington certainly thought so; it was he who had put the idea into Menteith's head.

"Get Stanford," Lord Wellington had written. "If there's a traitor at the war office, Stanford will find him."

Lord Menteith ran his eyes down the information listed in the file before him, trying to discover there the qualities that drew such confidence from Wellington. Adam Todd, Viscount Stanford, was the eldest son of the Earl of Dunstanburgh. Like many other scions of noble families he had gone out to the Peninsula as a cavalry officer and soon was appointed to Wellington's staff. It was not long before he became involved in the activity that had brought him his present reputation: intelligence work. His genius for penetrating deep behind enemy lines was unrivaled, and since he combined this ability with acute powers of observation he soon became invaluable to Wellington. "He is never wrong," the commander had said once. "Thanks to Stanford I know virtually the whole muster roll of all the opposing forces."

But this was intelligence work of a very different order, thought Lord Menteith. Still, the qualities that had made Stanford so effective in the field might be equally valuable in the quandary the Horse Guards now found itself in. At any rate Wellington certainly thought so.

Lord Menteith closed the file in sudden decision. He would send for Viscount Stanford.

Lieutenant Smeaton was relieved to see the bulk of Dunstanburgh Castle looming up before him. As he urged his horse on through the chill wind blowing off the water, he stared with a mixture of appreciation and horror at the huge fourteenth-century castle he was approaching. The appreciation was for its impressive bulk; the horror was at the thought that anyone actually lived here.

Dunstanburgh Castle was perched on a hill overlooking the North Sea. Its purpose when it had been built by the Normans was to guard the Northumberland coast, and, Lieutenant Smeaton thought as he regarded the faint marks of cannonballs on the walls, it looked as if it had done just that. Those outer walls were ten feet thick, and once Lieutenant Smeaton had passed into the courtyard he was confronted by a complex of seven enormous towers linked together by walls. He was met at the great door by an impressively correct majordomo who ushered him into the great hall, a room at least sixty feet in length and decorated with tapestries and a magnificent display of arms and armor.

"A message for Lord Stanford from the military secretary," the majordomo repeated, his voice expressionless. "If you will wait in the library, lieutenant, I will have his lordship informed of your arrival." Lieutenant Smeaton followed the servant into a huge, book-lined room with a fine vaulted ceiling. There was a fire roaring in the fireplace, and the frozen lieutenant went instantly to stand before it. The door closed behind the majordomo, and the lieutenant was left to thaw out as best he could while he waited for the appearance of a man he was keenly anxious to see. He had been hearing stories about Stanford for over two years now, and with the passion of youth—Lieutenant Smeaton was nineteen—he had made the young viscount his own personal hero. Suddenly, alone in this enormously impressive room, he wished he had not come. There was no one in real life who could measure up to what he had heard and imagined of Major Lord Stanford.

Adam Todd was walking on top of the old battlements of Dunstanburgh Castle when Lord Menteith's messenger arrived. He had been walking there, grimly, every day for the last two weeks, trying to build up the endurance of a badly injured leg. When the servant sent to find him arrived, he was leaning against the high stone wall looking out to the crashing sea below him. At the sound of his name he turned, black hair blowing in the early December wind.

"There is a messenger from London with a letter for you, my lord. From the Horse Guards."

Stanford's eyes widened slightly in surprise, the brilliant blue startling against the darkness of his hair and lashes. "I'll come immediately," he said in a cool, pleasant voice. Grasping an elegant stick in his right hand, he crossed the stone walkway to the door. It took him quite a long while to descend the stairs, and he was sweating slightly in the chilly stone hallway. The servant had not made the mistake of offering assistance.

Lieutenant Smeaton turned as the door opened, his greenish eyes bright with expectation and anxiety. He saw a slender, black-haired young man of medium height whose weight was very obviously resting on the stick he carried. Slowly Stanford crossed the room to the fireplace and lowered himself into one of the two chairs positioned there to absorb the heat and avoid the drafts. Only after he was seated did he extend his hand, and as he took it Lieutenant Smeaton noticed lines of pain around the firmly sculptured mouth of the man in the chair.

"Please sit down, Lieutenant Smeaton." Stanford gestured to the chair opposite his own. Then, when the young lieutenant was seated, he asked courteously, "What will you have to drink?" As Lieutenant Smeaton started to protest that he needed nothing, a liveried servant came to the door of the library. "Brandy, John," Stanford said.

The dense blue eyes, framed by very long, dark lashes, smiled at Lieutenant Smeaton. "Now, lieutenant," Stanford said in his pleasant voice, "what can I do for you?"

"I bear a message, my lord, from Lord Menteith. I was told to return with a reply."

Stanford frowned slightly. "May I have it?" He sat for some minutes reading, his thick black hair, grown longer during his illness, fallen over his forehead. He looked up at the lieutenant, and a flame showed, sudden and blue, in the depths of his eyes.

"You will stay the night, lieutenant," he said easily, "and I will give you an answer to take back in the morning."

"Very good, my lord," the young man said stiffly.

The brandy arrived then and he sat drinking a glass, listening to the easy voice of his host until a servant came to show him to his room. He was conducted up a stone staircase along huge drafty halls to a bedroom with a vaulted ceiling and a view of the crashing sea.

"Dinner is at seven, lieutenant," the servant told him. "I will come to show you the way."

Lieutenant Smeaton was thus left to himself for a few hours, to rest and to reflect on his impressions of Lord Stanford. He was the most handsome man Lieutenant Smeaton had ever seen, but that didn't account for the impression he made, the young officer thought as he looked out at the wild sea. Injured as he was, and obviously in pain, he still gave the impression of a man in total command of himself and of his world. It was impossible to imagine Adam Todd not succeeding at anything, once he had set his mind to it. Lieutenant Smeaton saw again in his mind's eye the firm, sensitive mouth and strong, slender hands of Viscount Stanford. I'd like to be like that, he thought wistfully, gazing at his own broad palms and thick fingers.

Stanford rested for an hour in the library before attempting the stairs to his room. He was lying, fully clothed, on his bed when the door opened to admit his father. Lord Dunstanburgh, the eighth earl, was a man nearing sixty whose only resemblance to his son had been the color of his hair, now turned gray. The earl's eyes were also blue, but a blue mixed with gray, and he was taller and heavier than his son.

"What is this I hear about a messenger from the Horse Guards?" he asked abruptly.

Stanford propped himself higher on his pillows and regarded his father peacefully. "They want me to come to London, sir. I'm to send a reply back with Lieutenant Smeaton in the morning."

"What?" Lord Dunstanburgh paced about the room in agitation. "Do you mean to tell me those fellows have the bloody gall to ask you to travel to London in your condition?"

Stanford grinned. He was well aware of his father's view of all things connected with the present government. In Lord Dunstanburgh's opinion there hadn't been a politician worth a damn since Charles Fox had died. "If I were feeling up to it, Papa," he said. "I think I should go."

"Nonsense, Adam." Lord Dunstanburgh came to stand next to the bed. His voice was rough with concern as he looked at his son's tired face. "You have been on your feet for only two weeks. You're not fit for a trip like that." He frowned suddenly. "What do they want you for, anyway?"

"Lord Menteith was not particular. He mentioned only a problem of security." Stanford's face became suddenly grim. "But I think I know what that problem is."

The look on Stanford's face startled Lord Dunstanburgh, and he thought, for the hundredth time since Adam had come home, that the boy had changed. The earl was intensely proud of him, but recognized that in his three years of absence Adam had passed far beyond his guidance. Nevertheless, he tried. "You don't belong at the Horse Guards. For that matter, you didn't belong in that ditch at Burgos."

"I've explained that to you, Papa," Stanford said patiently. "The weapons were inadequate and the troops demoralized. Soldiers hate siegework to begin with, and the attack on Burgos was woefully inefficient. Wellington needed all the officers he could get, and I happened to be there to report on some scouting assignment."

"The twins will be home soon for the Christmas holidays. They will be sorry not to see you."

"They saw me only a month ago, and I shall drive out to Cambridge to see them when they return. Besides, the Horse Guards will be pacific compared to a holiday spent with Matt and Nicky."

Lord Dunstanburgh smiled unwillingly. "There is some truth to that. If those young hellions make it through Cambridge I shall count myself fortunate." His mouth tightened. "I might as well save my breath, I suppose. Nothing I can say will keep you here, will it?"

The brilliant blue eyes smiled at him affectionately. "No, sir," Stanford said. "There is nothing you can say."

By the time Stanford reached the Clarendon Hotel in London he was thoroughly exhausted. At the last minute he had had an argument with his father over where he should stay. The Dunstanburghs no longer had a town house—the earl had given it up when his wife died—and he wanted Stanford to stay with his aunt, Lady Crosby. But since Lord Crosby, with his bosom friend Lord Holland, was a major Whig leader, Stanford did not think staying with his Aunt Frances would be at all politic. Lord Dunstanburgh did not agree, but when Stanford pointed out that the Crosbys were hardly likely to be in London in early December, he had reluctantly acquiesced in the Clarendon.

It was late afternoon when Stanford arrived. His leg hurt abominably. By the time he made it up the stairs to his room, sweat stung his eyes and his mouth was set grimly in pain. He went straight to bed, deciding to present himself to Lord Menteith on the morrow, if he survived the night.

A good night's sleep helped, though his leg still ached from the incessant jolting of the carriage. By the time he had eaten a very large breakfast and been helped by his valet to dress in a coat of black superfine, with cutaway tails, pantaloons, and Hessian boots, he felt equal to a trip to Whitehall.

Lord Menteith rose from behind his desk as Stanford entered and limped toward him. The military secretary held out his hand, noticed the stick grasped so firmly in Stanford's right hand, and let his own fall, unshaken. "Please be seated, Lord Stanford," he said in his deep voice. With a movement outwardly smooth, Stanford lowered himself into a large leather chair.

"I must thank you for coming so promptly, my lord," Lord Menteith began. "If the matter were not so urgent I should not have disturbed your convalescence, I assure you. How are you feeling?"

"Very well, I thank you," Stanford said in a quiet voice.

"Good." Menteith hesitated for a moment, unsure of

how to go on, and Stanford sat courteously waiting for him to continue. "The war against Napoleon is going well," Lord Menteith finally said. "The emperor has just announced to his nation the news of the annihilation of the grand army. He lost half a million men in Russia. He will be returning to Paris shortly, to begin recruiting anew."

"He has over three hundred thousand men in Spain he cannot touch," said Stanford.

"Precisely, Lord Stanford. For the first time Napoleon is seriously threatened on two fronts. The fighting this spring will be the most important offensive against Napoleon's power ever undertaken. Wellington must succeed!"

"I agree, Lord Menteith," said Stanford in his level, pleasant voice. "That is why I am here. You said something about a security problem?"

The broad-shouldered, brown-haired man behind the desk winced, then took a deep breath and said baldly, "We have a traitor at the Horse Guards, Stanford. And we need to find out who it is before he leaks the plans for the spring offensive."

Stanford's firm mouth tightened. "Are you sure he is here at the Horse Guards?"

"He must be," Menteith said in despair. "The importance and the detail of some of the information . . ." He shook his head. "It could only come from here."

"Do you have any suspicions as to who it is?"

Lord Menteith ran his hand through his hair. "No."

Stanford's hands were folded loosely on the top of his stick. "Your news does not come as a great surprise to me, my lord," he said softly, his eyes on his hands. "It has been obvious for some time that the French are more knowledgeable of our plans than simply several captured dispatches can account for." There was silence in the room as Stanford regarded his hands, his eyes shielded by his lashes. "You want me to find the man," he said evenly.

Menteith looked from the strong, slender hands lying so quietly on the stick to the still and reserved face above them. "Yes, I do," he said firmly.

Stanford looked up, and the dense blue of his eyes met Lord Menteith's worried brown ones. "I shall need your total cooperation," he said.

"Of course."

"Good. Let us start right now," Stanford said pleasantly, and for the next half hour he conducted an exhaustive interrogation of the military secretary which covered every aspect of life at the Horse Guards. It left Lord Menteith limp but relieved; he had turned his problem over to a professional.

Stanford even had thought of providing himself with a reason for spending time at the Horse Guards. "You know the difficulty we have been having with the French codes, my lord," he said. "By the time someone deciphers them the information is useless. I should like, while I'm here, to train a staff of 'experts' whom we can send out to Lord Wellington."

Menteith smiled. "An excellent idea. Now we have only—"

"I beg your pardon for disturbing you, Robert, but I am on my way to Hartwell. Do you have any news I should impart?"

"Matthieu." Lord Menteith rose to his feet, and Stanford followed suit more slowly. "No, I have no messages for his majesty, but I am glad you stopped in. May I present Lord Stanford, who is on leave from the Peninsula." To Stanford he said, "His grace the Duc de Gacé."

Chapter 2

And then you may revolve what tales I have told you
Of courts, of princes, of the tricks in war. . . .
                              —*Cymbeline*, III, iii, 14-15

The man who had entered the room was quite tall, with a fine, narrow, extremely modeled face. He looked to be in his early forties, and his fair hair and gray eyes were unusual in a Frenchman. He nodded to Stanford and advanced one more step into the room. "I am pleased to meet you, Lord Stanford. Your name is, of course, familiar to anyone who reads the reports from the Peninsula." The finely arched brows rose a trifle and he looked at Menteith. "Dare I hope Lord Stanford is going to lend us his talents?"

"You are correct as usual, Matthieu. Lord Stanford has agreed to take charge of our decoding problem."

"I guarantee nothing, your grace," said Stanford in an expressionless voice. "But I did have some success with codes in the Peninsula."

Gacé's pale eyes rested on him speculatively. "Indeed," he said smoothly.

Stanford's leg ached badly, and he could feel his shirt sticking to his shoulder blades. Gacé had made no motion to ask them to resume their seats, and Stanford wondered how much longer he would be able to keep on his feet. He was damned, though, if he was going to ask this supercilious duc for permission to sit.

15

Menteith came to his rescue. Noticing the sudden pallor of Stanford's face, he said heartily, "Sit down, Lord Stanford. Matthieu, will you join us for a brandy?"

"No thank you, Robert," the light, precise voice of Gacé said. He did not sit. "Where are you staying, Lord Stanford?"

"I'm at the Clarendon at present. My father gave up our London house years ago, so I must look for lodgings, I suppose."

"Come and stay with us for a bit." Gacé smiled, and Stanford was suddenly conscious of the duc's considerable charm, directed now at him. "You are not well—wounded, in fact, in a cause we émigrés are closely concerned with. I and my wife would consider it an honor if you would make our house your home while you are in London."

There was a touch of incredulity in Menteith's voice. "Is Nanda back in London, then?" he asked.

"Yes. She and the children arrived two days ago from Scotland. There is smallpox in the village at Pennington, so she decided to come straight to London. Charles came with her. They brought your mother to Fanly for a visit with the Fleetwoods. I understand she will be coming to us for Christmas."

The duc turned once again to Stanford. "You will be much more comfortable at Gacé House than at an hotel, Lord Stanford. Please do accept my invitation."

There was a perceptible pause, then Stanford answered slowly, "You are very kind, your grace. I should be honored to be your guest."

"Excellent," said the duc in his superb, barely accented English. "We will expect you tomorrow morning."

"Thank you, your grace. Are you sure the duchesse will not mind?"

"Positive," said his grace Matthieu de Vaudobin, Duc de Gacé. "Robert," a nod, and he was gone.

Stanford turned slowly back to Lord Menteith and

said carefully, "Just who is the Duc de Gacé and why is he so eager for me to stay with him?"

Menteith's honest brown eyes were filled with surprise. "Gacé is an unofficial attaché to Louis XVIII. He is the acknowledged émigré leader in England. I have no idea why he invited you to stay with him, though I think it is a good idea." He glanced at Stanford's stick. "My own wife is in the country, or I would have invited you to stay with us." Menteith smiled ruefully. "When Helen is away, I fear I virtually live at my club."

Stanford's eyes darkened at the implication that he needed someone to take care of him, but he chose to ignore it. "You haven't told me what Gacé has to do with the Horse Guards. You didn't mention him earlier."

Lord Menteith sighed and leaned back in his chair. "Gacé is a protégé of Lord Liverpool. He acts as a sort of liaison between the English war effort and the French government in exile. He is on his way out to Hartwell now to see Louis XVIII, and he also corresponds closely with the Comte d'Artois, Louis' brother. It is Liverpool's idea to appear to be working with the French, to avoid the appearance of looking to conquer lands in Europe for ourselves." Lord Menteith laced his fingers together and regarded them closely. "Gacé is connected to the Bourbons by marriage. His first wife was the daughter of the Prince de Condé." Menteith looked up and his steady brown eyes met the brilliant blue ones of Stanford. "His second wife," said Lord Menteith, "is my sister."

Stanford's black head nodded in sudden comprehension. "So as well as being Lord Liverpool's protégé, Gacé is your brother-in-law."

"His being my brother-in-law has nothing to do with his position," Menteith snapped. "I was against the marriage from the start, and nothing subsequently has made me think it anything but a dreadful mistake."

Nothing changed in the reserved courtesy of Stanford's face, but Menteith, looking at him, suddenly said ruefully, "Damn, I don't know what made me say that. I am not usually quite so forthcoming about family matters."

Stanford smiled faintly. "Perhaps I provoked you a bit," he murmured. "But I am still intrigued by the unexpected invitation."

"I am afraid I can't help you," replied Menteith, "but I agree it is surprising. Gacé usually goes about with the air of a prince who has abdicated his throne and holds the whole world in contempt. I am astonished he even noticed you."

Stanford grinned and suddenly looked much younger. "You paint a delightful picture of my prospective visit," he said.

Menteith raised his eyebrows. "My dear boy, you will be the envy of every man in London. After all, you will be the guest of my sister Nanda."

Stanford sighed and tried to shift his leg to a more comfortable position. "You had better tell me all about it," he said resignedly.

"My sister Amanda is married to Gacé," Menteith replied obligingly. "She is twenty-three years younger than he. She married him, over my protests, when she was just eighteen. Gacé has one daughter, Virginie, by his first wife. Ginny is now ten. And he and Nanda have one son, Marc, who is now four." There was a pause, then Menteith added slowly, "That is really all there is to tell. It is not an unusual household. Gacé occupies himself with government business, and Nanda supervises the children and maintains an active social life."

"If it is not an unusual house, why, then, will my staying there make me the envy of every man in London?"

The older man smiled at him kindly. "You will see, Stanford. Soon enough."

Stanford remembered Menteith's words as he lay on his hotel bed that evening, trying to position his leg comfortably. Evidently the duchesse was a *femme fatale*, he thought wryly. Unfortunately, he was in no condition to appreciate a *femme fatale* at the moment. Nor did he want a ministering angel hovering over him. What he wanted was to be left alone to do his job. He had accepted Gacé's invitation because he had seen the shock on Menteith's face and had sensed an urgency under the duc's smooth manner. And if Menteith's sister was all he had implied she was, Stanford was more curious than ever to know why the Duc de Gacé had invited him to be his house guest.

Nanda de Vaudobin wondered the same thing when Gacé told her of the invitation over dinner that evening. She looked at him in deep surprise, and he smiled blandly back.

"It was a kind thing to do, Matthieu," she said in her low, slightly husky voice. "I have heard stories about Lord Stanford, of course. Robert said Wellington was in despair over losing him, especially now that the war is finally going well. What is he going to do at the Horse Guards?"

"Decoding, according to Menteith. I don't doubt myself that he will be involved in the planning of the spring offensive."

"Probably." She hesitated, then said, "Has he completely recovered from his wounds?"

"No, he looked to be in some pain, which is why I invited him here. You will take much better care of him, *ma belle*, than they ever would at Clarendon's. He is to come around tomorrow morning."

"It is fortunate that I happened to be in London," she said. "This is the first Christmas we will not be spending at Pennington."

"Well, you could hardly have gone to Pennington with smallpox in the village."

"No." There was a pause, then she said carefully, "Well, it was a thoughtful gesture on your part, Matthieu, to invite him to stay with us."

"Thank you, my dear." Then, as she continued to look at him in wonder, "My dear Nanda, do not look so astonished. Give me credit for a sincere wish to be of service to someone who has done so much to serve the cause of Royalist France."

Her lashes lowered to screen her eyes. "Of course I do, Matthieu," she said gently.

And perhaps that did explain it, she thought later after she had read Marc his book and kissed Ginny goodnight. She was seated in the drawing room waiting for her brother Charles, who had promised to escort her to a party.

It was difficult for Matthieu, she told herself for perhaps the thousandth time. He had been forced to leave France when he was twenty-one years of age, and in twenty-four years of living first in Germany and then in England he had never reconciled himself to exile. Compared to many émigrés, Gacé was fortunate, Nanda thought. His father had been one of the few aristocrats to read the signs of the coming storm, with the result that he had sent most of his money and a great number of his valuables out of France before it was too late.

Matthieu had waited in France until his own life was directly imperiled and then had escaped to Germany disguised as a peasant. By the time he reached Baden his father was dead and he was the Duc de Gacé. But the Château de Gacé, which Nanda was familiar with through pictures and Matthieu's loving descriptions, was in alien hands. Its beauty and its location on the bend where the river Maine met the Loire saved it from destruction. It was taken over first by the local mayor, then in 1806 it had passed to the minister of finance, who still held it.

The one aim in Gacé's life was to recover the château,

property of the de Vaudobins since the fifteenth century. It was an obsession with him, Nanda thought unhappily. It made him incapable of finding satisfaction in anything else: not in his marriage to the daughter of a royal prince, not in his marriage to her.

Gacé's obsession so circumscribed his life that when he did something outside his usual rigid circle of friends and activities she found herself shocked. This invitation to Lord Stanford, who was a total stranger to them, surprised her deeply. It was clear, however, that he expected her to exert herself on behalf of the young man. Nanda, who valued greatly the equilibrium she had managed to achieve in her marriage, resolved to do just that.

The arrival of her brother Charles broke her train of thought. She turned to smile at his handsome, dark-eyed face, in many ways so similar to her own. "Survived the journey all right I see, Nan," he said easily. "How are the children?"

"They are just fine, Charles," she answered absently.

"Where is Gacé this evening that I have been pressed into service as an escort?" he asked her. The Honorable Charles Doune, one of Nanda's five brothers, had, like the rest of his family, a deep affection for his only sister. He was twenty-eight years of age and a member of Parliament for the family borough. He was in town at present, as he was a junior member of Lord Liverpool's government and was helping prepare for the opening of Parliament in January.

"Matthieu went to White's, I believe," Nanda replied with reserve. "Kitty Jermyn is giving the party this evening for those unfortunates like ourselves who have to be in London in December. But she is not one of Matthieu's favorite people."

"Not highborn enough for him, eh?" said Charles cynically. He was well acquainted with his brother-in-law's foibles.

"That is not the only reason Matthieu does not approve of her. However, I have always found her to have a very kind heart, so I promised to go." She walked to the door, then turned, a slight frown creasing her clear, wide brow. "The strangest thing has happened, Charles. Matthieu has invited Lord Stanford to stay with us while he does some work for Robert at the Horse Guards."

"Stanford? I thought he was badly wounded at Burgos."

"He was. But apparently he is well enough to do a desk job at present."

"And Gacé invited him to stay with you? That *is* peculiar." As he prepared to follow her out the door, he muttered again to himself, "Damned peculiar. Wonder what the fellow's up to?"

Chapter 3

I love and hate her: for she's fair and royal,
And that she hath all courtly parts more exquisite
Than lady, ladies, woman. . . .

—*Cymbeline*, III, v, 70-73

Stanford arrived at Gacé House in Berkeley Square at eleven o'clock the next morning. The butler had obviously been expecting him, and his luggage was swiftly removed from the carriage and sent, with his valet, to the bedroom he had been allotted.

"Will you come into the green saloon, my lord, and I will have her grace informed you have arrived? Or would you prefer to go straight to your room?" The butler scrupulously refrained from glancing at Stanford's stick.

"I will wait in the green saloon," Stanford said serenely and limped into a lovely room whose walls were covered with green silk hangings, making its name most appropriate. He sat down in a great velvet wing chair, his blue eyes on the tapestry that hung over the fireplace. He had just decided that it was an authentic Gobelin when the door opened to admit a very young girl. Stanford rose to his feet. "Don't tell me that you're the Duchesse de Gacé," he said solemnly.

The little girl giggled. "Certainly not. I am Virginie de Vaudobin. Mama will be here in a minute, and she sent me to entertain you until she arrived." Virginie came to stand before him, and he could see that she did indeed look like Gacé's daughter. Her hair was ash-blond like her father's, and her features were as finely etched. But the eyes that looked out from beneath her clear arched brows were warm hazel and full of healthy curiosity. She was a lovely child and would one day be an extremely beautiful woman. "Would you like some tea?" she asked earnestly.

"Thank you," he said gravely, "I should very much like a cup of tea."

"Marc fell down and cut his lip," Ginny explained as the cups were brought. "It was bleeding a little, and he always makes such a scene when he sees his own blood." She sighed wearily. "Honestly, sometimes he's such a baby."

"How old is he?" Stanford inquired courteously.

"He's four," she said with as much indignation as if she had announced he were forty.

Stanford made noises of sympathy and understanding over his teacup which encouraged Ginny to greater disclosures about the problems of a four-year-old brother. She was well launched on her favorite topic when Nanda entered the room five minutes later.

The man rose as she came in, and she noticed that he needed the help of his stick to get out of the chair. "I am sorry I was not here to greet you myself, Lord Stanford," she said in her low-pitched voice, "but I had a minor crisis on my hands." She gestured to the little boy who was holding tightly to her hand.

Marc de Vaudobin, Comte de Gacé, was a well-built child with silky brown hair and large dark eyes. He wore nankeen trousers and a sky-blue coat, and his lip was red and slightly swollen. At the moment his dark eyes were fixed on his sister. "I want something to eat too," he said in a clear treble. "Mama, why has Ginny got tea? I want tea too."

"Marc," said Nanda in a voice that caught his attention, "where are your manners?"

Thus called to mind, the little boy bowed politely to Stanford, and his eyes found Stanford's stick. "Why are you carrying a stick, sir?" he asked in his clear, carrying voice. "Only people who are quite old use sticks."

"I hurt my leg, I am afraid, and I need it to help me walk," Stanford explained easily.

"Lord Stanford was in the war, Marc," Ginny said.

The little boy's eyes began to sparkle, "When I grow up I'm going to be a soldier," he told Stanford. "I'm going to shoot Napoleon. I'm going to shoot all his soldiers. Uncle Charles is going to teach me."

"Enough, Marc!" said Nanda in her low, vibrant voice. She stepped forward into a shaft of light from the window, and Stanford looked at her fully for the first time. He had never seen anyone quite so lovely, he thought dispassionately. Her shining dark hair, in defiance of the current mode for short curls, was drawn smoothly off her face. Her skin was pale olive, with a warm, dusky rose on lips and cheeks; her features were finely boned and clearly cut. But it was the eyes that caught and held one. Huge and brown and thickly lashed, full of light and dark, they illuminated her face.

"Matthieu mentioned that your leg was injured," she said matter-of-factly. "I have put you in the first bedroom. Can you manage the stairs?"

"Stairs are no problem, your grace," he lied coolly. "I am just a bit slow."

She looked at him gravely for a minute, then turned to her daughter. "Ginny, will you take Marc back to the nursery while I take Lord Stanford to his room?"

"Yes, Mama." The little girl held out her hand to her brother. "Come along, Marc."

He hung back. "Will you play soldiers with me, Ginny?" he asked sweetly.

Virginie's hazel eyes met Nanda's for a minute. "All right," she sighed, "just for a little while."

He put his hand in hers and his voice could be heard

as they left the room: "You can be Napoleon and I'll be Wellington."

Nanda shook her head in rueful amusement and turned to Stanford. "Unfortunately, Marc's nurse contracted a severe inflamation of the lungs while we were in Scotland and is at her sister's recuperating. I tried to get someone to take care of him until she returns, but Marc hates strange people around him. I am afraid he is enjoying quite a bit more freedom than he is usually allowed."

"They are both lovely children," he said.

She smiled at him, and the still loveliness of her face lit to heart-shattering beauty. Something flickered in his eyes, then died, and he looked at her with a carefully neutral expression.

"Thank you," she said in her low, musical voice. "I'll show you to your room now."

Obediently he followed her out the door and toward the wide staircase. She chatted easily all the way, demanding no response and making it easy for him to concentrate on the task of getting up the stairs. He reached the top, pleased with himself for his best performance yet, and she opened a door at the top of the hall and led him in. It was a warm, cheerful room, with the sun pouring in the window and a fire burning in the fireplace. "Lunch will be in an hour," Nanda said. "I suggest you settle in and rest a bit."

He said nothing, but his eyes, brilliant blue in his fine-drawn face, met hers with an unmistakable message. Once again she gave him that wonderful smile. "I have two children of my own, Lord Stanford. Rest assured, I have no intention of mothering *you*." The door closed behind her, and he limped to the nearest chair, an unwilling glint of amusement in his eyes.

Gacé joined them for lunch and insisted on escorting Stanford to the Horse Guards for the afternoon.

During the next few days Stanford investigated every area of the War Department and found himself appalled by the laxity of security he discovered. In a distinctly unpleasant interview with Lord Menteith he listed with clinical exactitude all the violations of security which he had uncovered. The acid ruthlessness of Stanford's tone brought anger to Lord Menteith's eyes.

"Dammit, Stanford." He slammed his hand on the desk. "We never dreamed one of our own people would turn traitor."

"Someone has been leaking vital information to the French for the last six months, yet you continued to run this office as if it were a club library." Stanford's voice was level and empty. He handed a sheet of paper to Lord Menteith. "If the informer is a subordinate, these measures will eliminate a large number of his opportunities."

"If the informer is a subordinate . . ." The words reverberated in the room, and Lord Menteith said carefully, "Do you think, Stanford . . ."

"I think only that the security surrounding the spring offensive must be maintained." He leaned forward and spoke intensely, his blue eyes hard. "The campaign Wellington has planned for the spring is imaginative, comprehensive, and irresistible. It will push the French out of Spain for good. But its success depends upon the vital factor of surprise."

Lord Menteith sustained that blue gaze for a moment, then heaved a sigh. "I know, Stanford. You are, unfortunately, correct in what you say about us. This office is run like a club." He picked up Stanford's list. "But it won't be any longer. We will do as you ask."

Stanford's days at the Horse Guards exhausted him more than he cared to admit. He made himself lie down for an hour before dinner, and during the first week of his stay at Gacé House he had returned to his bedroom by nine o'clock. Gacé, unfailingly courteous, had several times invited him to the library for a brandy. The duc's conversation was light and amusing, his charm very much in evidence. Stanford had the impression he was waiting for the right moment to say something. But what Gacé wanted from him was still a mystery.

Even if the duc had had no ulterior motive in inviting him to visit, Stanford was still glad he had come to Berkeley Square. The duchesse had made several attempts to concern herself with his welfare, but was sensitive enough to recognize his unspoken rejection. Their relationship was now marked by a civilized and undemanding courtesy.

What he liked best about Gacé House was the children. He had grown up in a closely knit family, himself the oldest of four boys. His youngest brothers, twins, were now in their first year at Cambridge, but Stanford remembered them best as fourteen-year-old schoolboys whose high spirits in many ways resembled four-year-old Marc's. He had been good with his young brothers and he was very good with the Gacé children. In a very short time he was their hero.

Nanda was well aware of the burgeoning friendship between Stanford and Ginny and Marc. She liked to see him with the children; his whole personality changed. With her he was aloof and self-possessed. When the children were around there was a spontaneity and mischievousness about him that made him seem younger, and much more human.

Stanford and Nanda were sitting in the drawing room after dinner one evening eight days after Stanford's arrival when Ginny's governess, Miss Braxton, brought in the children. As they heard the sound of Marc's voice on the stairs, Nanda turned to him. "Now is the chance for you to make your escape, Lord Stanford. Once Marc sees you, you are as good as caught."

He looked very elegant in his black coat and snowy waistcoat and shirt. His thick black hair, newly cut, gleamed in the firelight. "I like them," he said simply. "I had not realized how much I have missed the sight and sound of happy children."

At this, Marc galloped into the room, followed more sedately by Ginny and Miss Braxton. "I knew you'd be here, Adam!" he cried. "I told you he would, didn't I, Ginny?"

"You did, but there's no need to shout, Marc," said Ginny with careful dignity. "Good evening, Mama. Good evening, Adam."

"Good evening," Nanda replied faintly. She looked at Stanford, her eyebrows raised.

He grinned, looking suddenly much younger. "I asked the children to call me Adam," he explained to the question in her eyes.

"You can't play bat and ball with a lord, Mama," said Marc helpfully.

"Bat and ball?"

"Adam played ball with me and Ginny in the garden today. I hitted the ball over the fence, Mama. I hitted better than anyone."

"Marc, if you break another window Papa will be extremely angry," Nanda said hastily.

The little boy frowned, his full lips pouting and his chin indenting in a cleft identical to his mother's. The pleasant voice of Stanford said easily, "We were very careful, your grace."

"Yes, Mama," said Ginny eagerly. "Adam pitched and he made us hit toward the street and away from the house."

"A few passing tradesmen had to move rather hastily, but we did not regard that as a problem," murmured Stanford gravely.

Nanda's eyes were bright with exasperation. "Of course you didn't," she retorted. "Your leg was no problem either, I suppose. If you have a relapse it will be quite your own fault."

"I never have relapses," he said firmly.

She looked at him, her lips slightly compressed, then shook her head.

"Quite right," he said, lifting his eyes suddenly.

Nanda surveyed his composed face critically. "You think a lot of your self-possession, don't you?"

His gaze, faintly hostile, was level. "Yes."

"What does 'self-possession' mean, Mama?" There was a frown on Marc's face and she turned to him, a soothing reply ready to allay his obvious apprehension of the tension between his mother and his friend.

Later that night, alone in his room, Stanford tried to analyze for himself his wariness of Nanda de Vaudobin. He did not trust Gacé. Some primitive instinct told him there was more to Gacé than what appeared on the surface. It was the same instinct that had made him so effective in intelligence work, and he did not disregard it now. Indeed, it was the reason for his being at Gacé House in the first place.

He did not trust Gacé, and Nanda was Gacé's wife. On the surface there was smooth accord between the duc and the duchesse. It was, as far as an outsider could tell, a successful marriage. If he didn't trust Gacé, obviously he shouldn't trust Nanda.

On that note Stanford went to sleep and slept deeply until the morning. Nanda spent a more troubled night. She was not used to being rebuffed, and it was clear that Lord Stanford did not like her. What bothered her most was his refusal to see her as the person she was. If she had not seen the side of his personality he showed to the children she would not have greatly cared how he felt about her. But she had seen, and she found herself very much wanting the friendship he had bestowed so freely on Ginny and Marc. Thinking about it kept her awake for a good part of the night.

Chapter 4

All of her that is out of door most rich!
If she be furnished with a mind so rare,
She is alone the Arabian bird. . . .
                        —*Cymbeline*, I, vi, 15-17

Christmas was coming swiftly, and the Gacé household reverberated with anticipation. Ginny and Marc were the chief mood-setters. Nanda was looking forward to her mother's visit and occupied herself shopping and making out menus. Stanford and Gacé were the least affected. They still went each day to the Horse Guards and spent a number of cozy evenings together in the library of Gacé House.

Stanford was surprised by the extent of knowledge Gacé displayed on those quiet December evenings. There was little going on in Europe that Gacé did not know about intimately. "I have friends and relatives in every court and palace of Europe," Gacé had remarked lightly to Stanford's comment about his extensive knowledge. "They are all terrible gossips and they live with pen in hand, as it were. Sooner or later, I hear everything."

Stanford had the distinct impression that Gacé was pumping him for information. His conversation about the Peninsula war displayed, on the surface, only a natural interest, but Stanford, himself a master at interrogation, recognized some very skillful probing. His highly developed instinct for danger focused more closely on the duc.

31

The security precautions Stanford had recommended were being fully implemented at the Horse Guards, but those precautions could easily fail with a spy who functioned at the level of Gacé. He had no proof, Stanford told himself, only an uneasy feeling about Gacé. But it was a feeling he could not shake.

Two days before Christmas Nanda's mother arrived. Stanford liked the Dowager Lady Menteith immediately. She was small and delicately boned, with gray eyes and her daughter's smile. She had been having tea in the green saloon with Nanda when Stanford came into the hall, and Nanda, hearing his footsteps, had invited him in to meet her mother.

"I am so pleased to meet you, Lord Stanford," Lady Menteith said in her soft voice. "I knew your mother many years ago."

Stanford looked surprised, and Lady Menteith, handing him a cup of tea, smiled. "Yes, I grew up in Yorkshire too. Your mother was ten years younger than I, but Marleigh Manor was only a few miles from Lambeth Castle, my home. You look very much like her, I might say."

Stanford, who had very happy memories of his mother, smiled at Lady Menteith in genuine pleasure. "Grandmama knows everybody," announced Marc from the doorway. "Did your mother get dead, Adam?"

"Marc!" said Nanda in distress. "What are you doing here?"

"I came to see Grandmama," Marc said loftily to his mother. "I only asked you that, Adam," he explained earnestly to Stanford, "because most of the people Grandmama knows are dead."

Stanford threw back his head and shouted with laughter, and, after a stunned moment, Nanda and Lady Menteith joined in. "That's the most telling comment on my

age I've heard in a long time," Lady Menteith said ruefully, when she could catch her breath. "The honesty of
the young is often overwhelming."

"The honesty of Marc is often extremely rude," said
Nanda, and ruthlessly bore her son off to the upper
reaches of the house.

Lady Menteith's coming served to alleviate somewhat
the cool politeness between Stanford and Nanda. For her
part she was relieved to see that he didn't react with au-
tomatic hostility to all women, and he found his liking
for Lady Menteith spilling over onto her daughter.

But it was not Lady Menteith who brought about the
major change in their relationship and forced Stanford to
admit he had made a mistake about Nanda. That realization had been coming for some time, but what crystal-
lized it was a set of architects' plans.

It was four days after Christmas when Stanford came
home early from Whitehall one day and entered the
green saloon to find the rosewood writing table covered
with drawings. On the small tea table was a sheet of
mathematical computations. Stanford picked them up
and went to stand next to the drawings. He was absorbed in looking at the two when the door opened quietly and Nanda came in.

"I see you are looking at my plans," she said.

Surprised, he turned and she came across the room to
stand beside him. "It looks like you are undertaking
some restoration work," he remarked.

She gave him a pleased smile. "Yes. Pennington is a
lovely Elizabethan house, but it was in sad disrepair
when Matthieu bought it. One of the wings needs extensive work; it needs to be rebuilt, in fact. But I want to
retain the Elizabethan style and at the same time enlarge
it. It has proved to be very complicated."

"Why?"

"Oh, we don't want to disturb the main section of the house—the towers, gables, chimneys, and so on. And it must *look* right."

"Who is your architect?" Stanford asked curiously. "These plans look very good to me."

"Yes, I think I have finally got it put together properly."

"How are you coming off of here?" He pointed to the north wall of the main part of the house.

"I'll show you." She picked up a pen and in a few minutes of technical description and mathematical computation she did indeed demonstrate how the problem he was alluding to could be solved.

When she finally put her pen down and turned to look at him it was to find him staring at her with a strange expression on his face. "You've done these plans yourself," he said slowly.

She smiled slightly. "Yes. I wasn't satisfied with any of the architects I talked to. They are only interested in creating their own style, not in restoring something of the past."

He looked again at the sheet of mathematics. They had not been done by the graduate of a fashionable seminary for young ladies.

"Who was your instructor?" he asked.

She didn't pretend not to understand him. "Michael Overbury." She began to fold the drawings up.

"Michael Overbury? The mathematician?"

"Yes." A drawing fell on the floor, and he bent to pick it up. Her eyes were serene as she took it from him. Nothing about her face suggested that she had said anything unusual.

He looked once again at the sheet of paper on the table. "How did one of the finest mathematicians in the world come to teach you how to do that?" he asked softly.

"My brother Charles took a course from him at the

University of Edinburgh, and he used to come to us for dinner and visits. I think . . ." The corners of her mouth deepened. "I think he was interested in Mother. Anyway, we were building a new house near Linlithgow at the time, and I was fascinated by it. Master Overbury taught me about plans, and how to calculate for stress, and things like that." A wicked gleam shone in her eyes. "He said I had a good brain."

"He was right," Stanford answered briefly, his eyes on the beautiful face so close beside him.

Later, after she had gone to a party, he sat in the quiet drawing room watching the fire die down and reassessing his image of the Duchesse de Gacé. There was more to her than her lovely face, obviously. He had been on guard against her ever since he had arrived in her home. No, before that even, he realized. He had been wary ever since Menteith had mentioned his sister's effect on men.

She had surprised him. Her beauty was indeed stunning, but there was some other quality she possessed which made her so extraordinary. He had felt her attraction immediately, and had been careful to keep himself at a distance. She used no arts to attract, she just did, and Stanford was shrewd enough to realize that she could be extremely dangerous. Beautiful, warm-hearted, shallow women always were.

That was what he had thought her: a shallow woman. She was married to Gacé, and she appeared happy in that marriage. No sensitive, deep-feeling woman could be happy married to a cold fish like Gacé.

Her architectural plans had stunned him. They were not the drawings of a society woman. They were professional. And the brain that Michael Overbury had seen fit to instruct belonged to no empty-headed, semiconscious lady of fashion. His whole image of the lovely, soft-spoken duchesse was undergoing a radical change.

Just what, he wondered, was the truth of the Gacé

marriage? He remembered now Menteith's comment that the marriage was a dreadful mistake. He remembered Nanda's face on Christmas morning as she stood watching Marc and Ginny opening presents. There had been tenderness there, but a fierceness too. He remembered thinking that she looked like a tigress whose cubs were in danger.

The fire cracked and Stanford yawned suddenly. He got to his feet, his leg stiff with weariness. Seemingly there was more to the Gacé household than met the eye. He would have to observe more closely than he had been doing. On that resolution, he limped up the stairs to bed.

During the next few days Stanford watched Nanda carefully, and the conclusions he came to were ones he would have reached weeks earlier had he not been so busy guarding against her. The serenity of the Gacé household emanated from her, but for the first time Stanford asked himself what the cost of that serenity was.

Damningly, Lady Menteith did not like Gacé. Nor did Menteith. Nor did Charles Doune, who had spent Christmas Day with them at Berkeley Square. Nanda's whole family was obviously devoted to her. Why, then, if her husband made her happy, did they so dislike him? The answer, Stanford thought, was obvious.

Why, then, did she stay with him? Her family would clearly support any separation effort she might initiate.

The answer to that question was also obvious, Stanford thought. Gacé had the children. If there was a divorce there was always the possibility of Nanda's winning custody of Marc, but she would have no claim to Virginie. Stanford thought now he understood that tender and fierce look he had seen on Nanda's face Christmas morning.

Chapter 5

I know not how a traitor.
—*Cymbeline*, V, v, 319

The more Stanford saw of Matthieu de Vaudobin the less he liked him. That his dislike of the duc was directly in proportion to his growing interest in the duchesse was something Stanford did not allow himself to contemplate.

One thing was certain: Stanford was becoming more and more convinced that the Duc de Gacé was the traitor he was looking for. For the past two weeks he had been reading the duc's mail. Gacé kept his correspondence locked in a desk drawer in his library at Gacé House, but Stanford had both the opportunity to spend time alone in the library and the skill to open an old-fashioned lock.

He found much what he had expected to find: Gacé operated one of the finest intelligence networks in Europe. He had told Stanford the simple truth; he did indeed hear everything. There was information about the present Prussian-Russian negotiations that caused Stanford to purse his lips in a soundless whistle. Stanford's brother Edward, who was serving as a diplomatic attaché under Sir Robert Wilson in Russia, had not been able to discover this kind of information. Nor, so far as Stanford knew, had Gacé seen fit to communicate his knowledge to any members of the English government.

Discreetly, Stanford began making inquiries about the

duc. What he discovered only deepened his suspicions: Gacé had joined the Horse Guards in June of 1812, when his friend Lord Liverpool had become prime minister. It was in the summer of 1812 that the first really serious leaks to the French had begun.

What Stanford could not discover was a motive. Why would the Duc de Gacé, trusted adviser to French royalty, rich, respected by his own countrymen as well as by the nobility of England and of Europe, throw in his lot with Napoleon Bonaparte?

He got a possible answer to his question from Lord Menteith. Menteith had been replying to Stanford's questions about the duc's escape from France and his earlier years in Germany. "He almost lost his head to the guillotine, according to Nanda," Menteith said. "Couldn't bear to leave the family château, apparently."

"Whatever happened to the Château de Gacé?" Stanford asked curiously.

"Napoleon's minister of finance has it. He bought it from the government about fifteen years ago. Matthieu can't even speak of it. Nanda says that he lives only to get it back again."

Stanford laced his long fingers together. "Surely Gacé must know that even if the king is restored it will be impossible for him to return all the property of the nobles who have been exiled these twenty years and more."

Lord Menteith snorted. "Matthieu thinks he has the king twisted around his finger. I am sure such a thought has never occurred to him."

Stanford, who had a very high opinion of the duc's intelligence, did not agree. Gacé, he was quite sure, had evaluated all possibilities. Could he possibly have come to the conclusion that his best hope of retrieving the Château Gacé lay with Napoleon? If so, then Stanford finally had what had puzzled him most about the possibility of Gacé's being the traitor: a motive.

Ever since their discussion about her architectural plans Nanda had sensed a change in Stanford's attitude toward her. The barrier he had erected between them had fallen and in its place was a growing friendship.

With the reopening of Parliament many families returned to London, and Stanford found himself besieged by invitations. He had gone off to war immediately after leaving Cambridge, so this was his first introduction to the social world he belonged to by birthright.

From the moment he walked into Lady Worth's reception, accompanied by Nanda and Gacé, he was a marked man. Stanford was the season's catch on the marriage mart. He was the heir to an ancient earldom and comfortably rich in his own right. He would inherit, besides the title, properties in four counties and a handsome fortune. At twenty-six he would have been a good catch if he were dull and ordinary. He was, in fact, neither.

His effect on the young bloods of the ton was almost as startling as his impact on the ladies. Nanda, who was deriving a good deal of entertainment from Stanford's "debut," took care to point this out to him. "Do you notice how many aspiring young sprigs of fashion have discarded their high collars and intricate neckcloths in favor of the military look?" Nanda teased him one evening as they stood together for a brief moment at a dance. He had been her escort for the evening, as her brothers were busy elsewhere and Gacé thought the company beneath his notice. Her eyes were on the figure of Lord Cecil Hathaway as he crossed the floor toward the orchestra. Stanford suddenly frowned. "What the deuce is wrong with that fellow?" he asked. "Why is he walking in that odd fashion?"

Her rich laugh pealed out. "He is limping," she gasped, when she could speak again. "It is all the crack, you know."

He turned to her, incredulous laughter flaring in his eyes. "Are you serious?"

The delight in her eyes and smile drew him closer to her, unconscious even that he had moved. "I swear it," she said.

"Your grace, I believe you promised me this dance." The smooth voice belonged to the Marquess of Rockingham, whose jealous eyes went from Nanda's face to Stanford's.

"So I did, my lord," she answered, the ghost of a chuckle still in her throat. She moved out onto the floor, followed by Rockingham, and Stanford stood still for a moment watching her.

The light from the great chandelier above drew gleams from her dark hair and illuminated the clear skin and fine features of her face. She wore a gown of palest rose gauze over an underdress of ivory satin. Her eyes shone like candles; you could warm your hands at her, he thought suddenly.

"How are you, Stanford?" said a deep voice next to him, and he turned to see the Honorable Charles Doune, Nanda's brother. Charles was closest in age to Nanda of all her brothers; he was twenty-eight. And he was unmarried, so Nanda occasionally pressed him into service as an escort when Gacé was not available. He and Stanford had met numerous times; he liked Stanford in about the same degree as he disliked Gacé.

"The House session over, Doune?" Stanford asked easily.

"Not yet. But a few croakers got started on Wellington, and I couldn't sit there any longer. Thought I'd look in here before going on to White's." His eyes followed his sister for a moment, then he said, "Where's his grace tonight? Too ramshackle an affair for him to lend his presence, eh?"

Stanford said nothing, and Charles cast a sapient eye his way. "No need to be discreet, man. I've had Gacé pegged since first I met him. Pity of it is, Nanda wouldn't believe me. Had it in her head he was some kind of martyr, lonely and sorrowful and noble. Well, you know Nanda. It was a bait she couldn't refuse."

Stanford's face was composed, his voice quiet. "How was your sister allowed to marry him if your feelings about him were so negative? I gather that Lord Menteith shares your opinion of the duc."

Charles heaved a sigh. "My mother, of course. Gacé charmed her too. Robert might have held out against one of them, but combined they put him to rout. He consented and they were married. My mother changed her mind about the duc, but unfortunately it was too late. And, of course, it is a point of honor with Nanda to keep a good face on her marriage." He finished the champagne in his glass, put it down and looked once again at his sister as she smiled at something Lord Rockingham had said to her. "I have never liked anything less," he said grimly. "And there's not a damn thing I can do."

Stanford drew a careful breath and said, in a perfectly controlled voice, "Why do you dislike Gacé so intensely, Doune? Is it just his excessive pride?"

Charles frowned and reached for his champagne glass. He frowned at its emptiness for a minute and said, "Damn," but without any heat. "I'm not exactly sure," he answered finally. "There is something, well, inhuman about him. One ought to feel a relationship to things, to other people. I don't think Gacé does that. His colossal egotism recognizes only one thing: the superiority, the rights, the needs, of Matthieu de Vaudobin. His wife, his children, only exist for him insofar as they are a mirror of his own self-esteem." He laughed, and the sound was distinctly unpleasant. "Poor little Ginny. You should have seen her before Nanda took her in hand. 'Yes, Papa,' 'No, Papa,' afraid to breathe because Papa might not approve of the way she did it."

Stanford suddenly felt exhausted; his leg hurt abominably. In a voice flat with fatigue, he said, "There is one other thing, surely, besides himself that Gacé is devoted to."

Charles' brown eyes regarded him skeptically. "And what is that, Stanford?"

"The restoration of the French monarchy."

There was silence for perhaps five seconds, then Charles said slowly, "I shouldn't be so sure of that, Stanford. In Gacé's mind the restoration of his own lands and prestige far outweighs the restoration of the Bourbons. The monarchy is, like everything else, valuable to Gacé because it is useful to him." A smile suddenly lit his handsome face. "How are you, old girl?" he said affectionately to his sister as she joined them.

"Fine!" she retorted. "No thanks to you. I thought you were engaged this evening."

"So I was. And now I am unengaged."

"Well, I would feel sorry for Lord Stanford for having to escort me if I hadn't seen him deftly cutting out Lord Oxridge and poor Mr. Charlton with Miss Marrenby. Took her off to supper right under their noses. They will be limping in earnest by tomorrow."

"The Marrenby, eh?" said Charles appreciatively. "Good for you, Stanford. The looks of an angel, and money too."

Stanford, unreasonably, was annoyed at their gentle teasing. "I'm not at the altar quite yet," he snapped.

Nanda looked at him quickly, seeing how drawn and tired he looked. She stifled a yawn and said, "I am more than ready to leave, if I may prevail upon one of you gentlemen to see me home."

Stanford's dense blue eyes met hers in perfect comprehension, but the studied innocence of her face effectively dissipated his resistance. "Oh, very well," he said, somewhat ungraciously. "Let us go."

As he limped off to get her cloak, Charles turned to

his sister, eyebrows raised. A light danced in the depths of her eyes. "I am not tired, Charles," she said, her voice carefully uninflected.

"Oh." He looked toward the door. "Doesn't like to admit it, eh?"

"No," she said gently.

"He's a good man, Stanford. I like him."

"Yes." She hesitated. "I do too."

In ten minutes they were in the Gacé carriage on their way home to Berkeley Square, where Stanford was to spend a sleepless night turning over in his mind the things he had heard from Charles.

Chapter 6

Your lady
Is one of the fairest that I have looked upon.
—*Cymbeline*, II, iv, 31-32

Stanford paid a visit to an old friend the day after his conversation with Charles Doune. Mr. Joseph Bottoms had served Stanford in the Peninsula until he had been wounded last January at Ciudad Rodrigo. Stanford had bought a tavern on Fleet Street, which he had turned over to Mr. Bottoms on terms so generous as to make it an outright gift. It was to the Green Oak that he repaired early the next morning for a private conversation with ex-Sergeant Bottoms.

"Damn, but its good to see you, my lord!" Bottoms said, his florid face bright with pleasure. "I see your leg's on the mend. No more cane, eh?" They were sitting in a small private room at the rear of the tavern. Bottoms had taken Stanford there as soon as he had indicated that he wished to be private. They sat now facing each other across a scarred wooden table, two tankards in front of them.

"Yes, I am doing very well, Joe," Stanford answered. "I was luckier than you were."

"Oh, I don't know, my lord. If it hadn't been for this"—he gestured to the empty sleeve that was pinned across his chest—"I wouldn't be here, all snug and tidy, and about to get married in the bargain."

A delighted smile crossed Stanford's face. "Good for you, Joe! Who is the lucky woman?"

"Her name is Hetty James. Her pa owns the stable on the next street. But you didn't come here to listen to me run on like a bloody don, my lord. What can I do for you?"

Stanford frowned. "It is a rather delicate business, Joe. What we arrange this morning must go no farther than this room."

Bottoms looked impassively at the young man seated across the table from him. The thick black hair fell slightly forward across Stanford's forehead, and there were long shadows under his cheekbones and an unaccustomed tightness to the set of his mouth. For the first time Bottoms recognized how much older he looked. He dropped the sarcastic remark that had been forming on his lips and said merely, "You have my word on it, my lord."

Stanford smiled. "Thank you." He leaned forward slightly. "Joe, I need two men to keep the Duc de Gacé under surveillance at all times. I want reports on where he goes, who he sees, what he does."

It was Bottoms' turn to frown. "The Duc de Gacé? Isn't that the cove you're staying with?"

"Yes."

"Something fishy about him, eh?"

"Very."

"It don't suprise me at all," said Bottoms knowledgeably. "He's a frog, ain't he? They're all the same."

"Spare me your philosophy, Joe, I beg you," said Stanford, the ghost of a laugh in his voice. "Do you know anyone who can do it?"

"Oh, I think so, my lord."

"Good. I will want to see them, but don't give them my name. I shall be Mr.—ah—Devon."

"Very well, my lord."

Stanford looked at Bottoms' carefully expressionless

face. "I can't tell you what it is all about, Joe. And it is imperative that Gacé not be aware he is being followed."

"Don't you worry, my lord," Bottoms assured him. "The two men I have in mind could follow Boney to the privy and never be noticed."

Stanford grinned. "I'll leave it up to you, then, Joe. Have them here tomorrow at three and I'll give them their instructions."

"Very good, my lord."

After another pint of ale, and some more personal chat, Stanford left the Green Oak, slightly relieved to have taken some positive action about a problem that scared him to death.

He went immediately to the Horse Guards, where he spent several hours coping with the masses of paperwork lying on his desk. Gacé had not been wrong when he had surmised that Stanford would be involved in the planning for Wellington's spring campaign. He had done some important scouting for Wellington last autumn, before he was wounded, so he was aware both of the commander's plans and of what was needed to implement them.

The first problem confronting London was that an enormously cumbersome bridging train had to be brought from the Tagus River to the Douro, without the enemy realizing it was being moved. Wellington's plan was to lead a decoy army of thirty thousand men along the Salamanca road while the real invasion force of sixty thousand marched secretly through the wilderness of Trás os Montes, country the French thought impassable. Stanford knew it was not impassable, having scouted it himself. The army would cross over the transported bridge, thus outflanking the French.

The second half of this brilliant campaign was what was engaging more and more of Stanford's attention.

Once the army was reunited at Toro, Wellington planned another jolting surprise. He would turn north, not east, aiming for the French border at the west end of the Pyrenees.

For this second maneuver to succeed, Wellington planned to abandon Lisbon and Oporto as supply bases and rely instead on Santander on the Bay of Biscay. Santander would be provisioned by ships from the Royal Navy, using the short sea route from England. Close cooperation between the army and the navy was essential for the success of the campaign, and it was in this delicate operation that Stanford was being increasingly employed. The masses of paperwork on his desk had chiefly to do with this latter problem.

But it was the problem of security that chiefly occupied Stanford's mind. If the French were given advance knowledge of Wellington's plans, the campaign was doomed. The fact that the government had called him in was a measure of its own concern. But he could hardly accuse someone as notable as the Duc de Gacé, bosom friend of Lord Liverpool, major support of Louis XVIII, connected to nobility all over Europe, without hard, verifiable proof. How to get that proof was the difficulty. A further problem he tried not to contemplate was the effect on Gacé's family if he was indeed successful in exposing the duc as a traitor.

Stanford's mind was still preoccupied with Gacé when he reached Berkeley Square. He was walking around from the stables, his black brows drawn together in concentration, when he heard the laughter of children. He looked up to see Ginny and Marc playing with a small dog in front of Gacé House. As he watched, the front door opened and Nanda, wearing only a walking dress, came out, her arms folded against the winter chill. As she reached the children the dog pulled away from Marc's hold and darted out into the cobbled street. In a flash Marc was after him.

At that moment a tilbury harnessed to a fast-moving bay swung into the square. With a cry Nanda flung herself into the street, dragging Marc from under the hooves of the oncoming horse and sheltering him with her own body. To the horrified Stanford it seemed as if the horse would surely trample on her. Then the bay reared up, swung to one side by the strong hands of the driver.

Nanda hardly heard the questions of the driver or Ginny's sobbing; she had eyes only for Marc. She was on her knees in the street, supporting him in her arms. He was unconscious, and blood was streaming down his face from a gash on his forehead.

A quiet voice said, "He hit his head on the cobbles when you pushed him. He knocked himself out, that's all." A clean, folded handkerchief was put in her shaking hand. "Hold that over the cut."

Her eyes met the steady, reassuring ones of Stanford, then she nodded and pressed the handkerchief over the gash on Marc's forehead. Quickly and gently Stanford ran his hands over Marc's small, sturdy body, feeling for broken bones. "He's all right, I think," he said in the same quiet, steady voice. "Keep that handkerchief tight over his forehead, Nanda. I am going to carry him into the house. Ginny," he said over his shoulder to where she stood behind him, her hazel eyes dilated in horror, "run into the house and tell March to send for the doctor. Marc is going to need this cut stitched." She flew to obey him. Kneeling, he lifted the injured child smoothly into his arms, rose easily to his feet and walked up the stairs and into Gacé House, Nanda close by his side keeping the makeshift bandage in place.

"Bring him into the drawing room and put him on the sofa," she told him breathlessly. Marc was beginning to stir in Stanford's arms, and as he laid the child down Marc's lashes fluttered and his eyes opened. He saw his mother's strained face and immediately began to cry.

She bent over him. "It's all right, darling, Mama's here. Do you hurt anywhere, Marc?"

"My leg," he whimpered. "My leg hurts, Mama."

"Get me a knife," Stanford said curtly to the servants who stood wide-eyed in the doorway.

With the knife in his hand he proceeded to cut Marc's boot down the side, then eased it gently off his foot. The ankle was already swelling.

A knock sounded at the front door and in a moment the doctor came in. He spoke gently to Marc, who had begun to cry again, looked at his cut forehead, and said to Nanda, "This will have to be stitched."

At that Marc shrieked and Nanda's face went from white to alabaster. Stanford went to stand next to the boy. "Marc," he said. Something in his quiet voice caused the child to stop crying and look at him. "I am ashamed of you," Stanford said gravely. "I thought you had more bottom than this."

"I do have good bottom," Marc whispered, tears still running down his face.

"Then let me see it." Stanford bent closer to the little boy. "I know it hurts and I know you are frightened but, believe me, you are not badly injured. The doctor will be able to fix both your head and your leg if you will just cooperate and let him. If you let a little accident like this throw you, you will never make a soldier, you know."

Marc's brown eyes, so like his mother's, were fastened on Stanford's steady blue ones. He gritted his teeth. "Stitch it," he said heroically to the doctor. Then, with still the hint of a sob in his voice, "Will you hold my hand, Mama?"

"Of course I will, darling." She sat down on the floor beside him, his small, dirty hand grasped comfortingly in hers.

Stanford turned to put a comforting arm around Ginny. "Come, Ginny, let's you and me leave Marc to your mother and the doctor. Suppose we go upstairs to your sitting room and have a cup of tea."

He sat with Ginny and her governess for half an hour, then went back downstairs to his own room. He was sitting in front of the fireplace, a book in his hand, when there came a soft knock at the door. He opened it to find Nanda. "I just came to tell you Marc is all right—sleeping, in fact. His ankle isn't broken, only sprained."

She still wore the dress she had had on earlier, but now it was stained with Marc's blood and dirt from the road. A few long strands of hair had come out of her chignon, and there was dirt on her cheek and her nose. In a voice that was suddenly unsteady she said, "Thank you, Adam. You were a great help."

He reached out, took her arm, and steered her into the room to the chair where he had just been sitting. "Sit down," he said briskly. Then, as she hesitated, "Don't worry, I'll leave the door open. It will all be perfectly proper." With a shaken laugh she dropped into the chair, then bent to put her head down on her lap.

He leaned his shoulders against the mantel, watching her but saying nothing. When she raised her head she was still pale, but the momentary faintness had passed. Her great eyes met Stanford's, a curious gravity in them. "I don't know why I had to save that for you."

"You were upset," he said in an expressionless voice. "It was a natural reaction."

Suddenly she smiled. "You are too damn competent, that's the problem. It makes one tend to relax one's own efforts, to let down."

"Is that such a bad thing?"

She thought for a minute. "Yes, it is," she said slowly. She rose to her feet. "It is always dangerous to grow too dependent."

She stood before him, slender and disheveled as a child, but the expression in her eyes was not at all child-like. She was so close he could feel the warmth of her skin. They looked at each other for a long minute, then Nanda turned and walked to the door. Into the silence of the room she said steadily, "Thank you, Adam, for all your help this afternoon." She stepped into the hall and closed the door firmly behind her.

Chapter 7

Disloyal! No:
She's punished for her truth, and undergoes,
More goddesslike than wifelike, such assaults
As would take in some virtue.

—*Cymbeline*, III, ii, 6-9

When Nanda came down to the breakfast parlor the next morning she found Stanford still at the table. She had had an uncomfortable night and had awakened with a nagging headache. The sight of Stanford brought back to her the reason for her sleeplessness. She had spoken the truth when she had told him she feared becoming dependent on him. The bitter lesson her marriage had taught her was to depend on no one but herself. Adam—Lord Stanford!—was a delightful friend to have, she told herself sternly, but she must not get used to having him around. No one must be allowed to weaken her ability to shoulder the responsibility for her children. And it was only too easy, she acknowledged bitterly, to allow herself the luxury of leaning on someone else's strength. She rubbed the aching muscles in the back of her neck and went to pour herself a cup of coffee.

"Good morning, Lord Stanford," she said lightly.

He looked up from his newspaper, black brows raised in surprise. "Yesterday you called me Adam," he said. "Have I done something to deserve being relegated back to Lord Stanford?"

The brown eyes regarding him looked faintly affronted. "Has anyone ever told you you have no tact?" she asked.

52

"Never," he said solemnly.

"I don't believe you."

"Don't you want to be on a Christian-name basis with me?" he inquired. "If you don't, just say so."

She looked critically at his politely questioning face, put her cup down, looked again, and then, reluctantly, her wonderful smile broke out. "You're impossible," she said. "Adam."

Stanford went to the Horse Guards feeling he had successfully weathered a minor crisis. He had known very well what Nanda was telling him by her formal salutation and had chosen, for reasons he didn't bother to define, to challenge it. She was a thoroughly nice person, he told himself. It was pointless to go back to the careful civility of their earlier relationship for a senseless scruple on her part. There was no reason in the world why they could not continue to be friends.

He spent the morning dealing with a problem that had been brought to his attention by the Admiralty. As he was writing out a last order the door opened and Gacé stood on the threshold.

"I hope I am not disturbing you, Stanford," the duc said in his precise English.

"Not at all, Gacé." Stanford put down his pen and rose to his feet. "Please do come in."

Gacé closed the door behind him and crossed the room to Stanford's desk. His cool gray eyes took in the neat pile of maps and plans and papers. "You are an example to us all, dear boy, with your dedication and your industry."

Something flickered in Stanford's blue eyes, but he said merely, "Thank you." He quickly scanned his desk to make sure nothing of importance was visible and said, "Won't you sit down, Gacé?"

"Thank you." Calmly the duc seated himself, his eyes

on Stanford's face. "I have come first of all to thank you for your assistance to my wife and son yesterday."

"I was glad to be of service, Gacé, but your wife was the heroine of the day. She saved Marc from serious injury."

Gacé's face darkened. "Marc is sadly in need of stronger discipline. Unfortunately, my wife is incapable of understanding this."

"I don't believe I've ever seen a more devoted mother than her grace," Stanford said pleasantly.

Gacé's gray eyes narrowed momentarily, but Stanford's face remained politely aloof. "I have conceded the battle of the children," the duc said finally. "They are my wife's concern. As you say, she is very fond of them." There was a pause, then Gacé said carefully, "I am on my way to Hartwell, Stanford. The king is alarmed because England has refused to commit troops to Germany. Have you any suggestions as to what I may say to him?"

Stanford picked up a pen and regarded it thoughtfully. "Baron Stein assured us that the nationalistic mood in Germany at present resembles that in Spain. If that is so, surely Prussia and Austria are the natural leaders in that part of the world."

"The king has seen Prussia and Austria fall to Napoleon too often to put much faith in their effectiveness," Gacé said smoothly.

Stanford's eyes were guileless as he smiled at the duc. He turned the pen over and over in his long fingers. "Between you and me, Gacé," he said softly, "I think things will go very differently this time."

"Why?" There was a frown between the duc's fair brows.

"The Prussians are going to sign a treaty with Russia."

"How do you know that?" Gacé's voice was sharp.

From your letters, Stanford wanted to answer, but refrained. "Surely it must be obvious to any person of sense," he substituted. "General Yorck's action at Tauroggen makes it almost inevitable."

"Perhaps." Gacé was noncommittal. "But the Prussians hardly have what one would call a good army. Certainly not one that can withstand Napoleon."

This was indisputably true, but it was not Stanford's policy to reassure Gacé. "Boney's own army is not as well trained as previously," he pointed out. "The veteran forces that remain after the Russian debacle are all held down in Spain."

"It is not the grand army, I grant you, but Napoleon still has a better army than the Prussians."

"Possibly. But I doubt if Boney could face the combined forces of Russia, Prussia, Austria, and the states of the Rhenish Confederation."

"Metternich is not going to commit Austria." Gacé's voice was tight. "And if Austria remains neutral, Bavaria and Baden will also."

Stanford's eyes narrowed. He was smiling, and Gacé did not like that smile at all. "If I were Napoleon, Gacé, I shouldn't count on that."

There was a long pause, then Gacé said slowly, "Well, you are certainly encouraging, Stanford. I shall pass your words along to his majesty."

"By all means, Gacé, if you think they will help reassure him."

The duc rose to his feet, and Stanford rose with him. "I imagine what happens in Spain this spring will have a very strong bearing on the events in Germany," Gacé said slowly.

"I should certainly think so," Stanford replied truthfully.

Gacé walked to the door, then turned once again. "By the way, Stanford, I may be detained overnight at Hartwell, and there is a reception this evening at Carlton House I was to have taken my wife to. I fear now I shall

be unable to attend. I was wondering if perhaps you
. . . ?" Delicately, Gacé left the question hanging.

"I should be delighted to escort the duchesse, Gacé,"
he said promptly.

"Excellent," Gacé put his hand on the doorknob. "I
don't know how we should get on without you, Stanford."

"Very well, I suspect. It is I who am grateful to you
for your kind hospitality." He hesitated, then said
slowly, his eyes on Gacé's face, "I won't be bothering
you for much longer, however. I have heard of some
good rooms near St. James's. I thought I'd go and have a
look at them this afternoon."

A look of genuine alarm flitted across Gacé's face,
leaving only solicitude and concern in its wake. "We
shall all be devastated if you leave us, Stanford," he said.
"Your stay in London is not going to last beyond the
summer, I am sure. There is little point in taking rooms
and engaging servants for a few months only. Remain
with us." He smiled, totally charming, totally at ease.
"My wife and my children would never forgive you if
you deserted us for a set of rooms, you know."

"You are very kind," Stanford said gravely.

"Not at all. I am really very selfish." Another
charming smile and Gacé was gone.

Stanford sat on at his desk until the dusk gathered
around him. "I am very selfish," Gacé had said, and
Stanford believed him. Why, then, was Gacé so anxious
to have him as a permanent house guest? It was odd, at
the very least, for a man like Gacé to introduce into his
home, into close contact with his wife, a man like himself. The only answer was that Gacé wanted something
from him and he was prepared to take the necessary
steps to get it.

When Gacé had first left Nanda to Stanford's escort
Stanford had thought perhaps the duc was trying to
seduce him through his wife. But as he got to know the

principals better he had seen the falseness of that idea. Nanda's reputation was flawless. What Menteith had told him was true: most of the men in London were in love with her. But in a town that talked about everybody and all the time, there was never any gossip about Nanda. If she hadn't succumbed to the blandishments of the most sophisticated men in London, there was no reason to suppose she would succumb to him.

There was, of course, every reason to suppose that he would succumb to her. Nanda's spell lay not only in her beauty but in the warmth of spirit that lay behind it. That was the light that danced in the darkness of her eyes, the radiance that illuminated her smile. Once a man got close to Nanda it was impossible to think of him voluntarily exiling himself.

Stanford was sure that Gacé had taken all these facts into his calculations. The duc did not love his wife. Stanford doubted that he loved anyone except himself. But he trusted her. No, Stanford thought, trust was the wrong word. He numbered her as one of his possessions, to be used as he needed her.

And he was using her now, to keep Stanford at Gacé House. It would please the duc very much if his young guest should fall in love with his wife. He wanted Stanford available, under his roof, so he could pick his brain at leisure, casually and charmingly, about the spring offensive.

There was a distinctly grim look about Stanford's mouth as he sat in front of his laden desk that bleak February afternoon. He had said enough to Gacé to shake the duc out of whatever complacency he might have been harboring. He had certainly made clear the importance of the Spanish campaign to Napoleon's future. It only remained for Stanford to follow up his opening move. For Stanford had never had any intention of leaving Gacé House. Not because of Nanda, he thought doggedly, but because of Nanda's husband.

Chapter 8

. . . abide the change of time,
Quake in the present winter's state and wish
That warmer days would come. . . .

—*Cymbeline*, II, iv, 4-6

As it turned out Nanda did not attend the regent's reception. The headache she had awakened with had grown worse as the day progressed until by evening it had become a full-scale migraine. She lay on her bed in a darkened bedroom, a wet rag soaked in vinegar on her forehead, and every bone in her head drummed with pain. Every hour Ginny faithfully appeared, bringing a newly soaked cloth. They didn't help, but Nanda accepted them because they gave Ginny something to do for her.

There was nothing anyone could do to alleviate the pain; this Nanda knew from past experience. She must just endure it until it receded of its own accord.

She was familiar with headaches. They had started about six months after her marriage. She could still recall her first real quarrel with Matthieu, when she had realized that his icy demeanor toward his daughter was quite deliberate, part, in fact, of his determination to force Ginny into the role of royal princess that he wanted her to play. Nanda had rebelled and soon discovered that she, too, was expected to fit into a role, that of adoring wife. She had not fit very well at all, and in despair she had watched Gacé's growing hostility toward her as she tried desperately to assert her own and Ginny's personal freedom.

As she lay on her bed in the darkened room that February night the sense of horror and suffocation she had felt then was suddenly vividly present to her once more. She had not known it was possible to be so bitterly unhappy. Matthieu was never violent. He was not cruel. It was simply that everything he valued, everything he stood for, was morally repugnant to her. He dwelt in the closed, stifling world of his own pride, and she could not breathe in its atmosphere.

She could not leave him, because of the children. And he could not bear the world to know that there was strife between him and his beautiful young wife. They had reached a compromise. Gacé had given her freedom to deal with the children in whatever way she wished. And she, for her part, made every effort to be the sort of wife he had expected her to be.

They had achieved a measure of content, or so she had thought. Her headaches had abated.

But now, as she lay suffering the pounding agony she had not known for over a year, she feared for the future. Matthieu had changed of late. There was a tautness about him that had not been there before. Perhaps that was the reason for her recent feeling of depression, she thought, lying still on her wide bed. It must be. Nothing else in her life had changed.

Stanford went to the reception alone. He was in no mood for the chatter and gossip of Carlton House, but his attendance was virtually a royal command. Ever since he had become regent, the prince had shown himself more friendly to Wellington and the Tories, and he had expressed an interest in meeting Stanford, the man Wellington had called his "eyes and ears."

Stanford did in fact spend some half an hour in conversation with the regent, whose good sense on the subject of the war somewhat surprised him. He thought that if the prince devoted only half the time he spent on his cronies and his romances to the business of government, he might prove to be an able king.

Carlton House was filled with government members and their families. Stanford saw Miss Marrenby, whose father was a member for Buckinghamshire, and made his way to her side.

"What a crush!" he said to her pleasantly. "May I get you a glass of champagne, Miss Marrenby?"

Elizabeth Marrenby turned to him, a smile on her lovely face. She was her father's only child and heiress to his considerable fortune. When they had first come to London last year, the Marrenbys, newly returned from India, had not known anyone in society and Elizabeth, for all her divine good looks, was in danger of being ignored. None of the great hostesses deigned to invite her to their parties, and she certainly was not going to be given vouchers for Almack's.

Nanda had met her at a milliner's in Bond Street one morning and, falling into conversation, had taken a liking to the girl. Under her lovely exterior Elizabeth had a genuinely sweet nature, and Nanda kindly included her in several of her own schemes. Once it was seen that the Duchesse de Gacé had given her seal of approval to Miss Marrenby, others were swift to follow. From a nonentity Elizabeth soon became one of the acknowledged successes of the season.

Nanda had introduced Stanford to her, and Elizabeth had taken an instant liking to the beautiful, black-haired young man with the limp. No matter how besieged by admirers she might be, she always made time for Lord Stanford, even though his injury made it impossible for him to dance.

Mrs. Marrenby watched Stanford's black head, bent now in easy conversation toward the golden curls of her daughter, and there was a gleam of complacency in her eyes. She would very much like to see her daughter become a countess, and Stanford was heir to the Earldom of Dunstanburgh. Pleased with her thoughts, she smiled with gracious compassion at a passing turbaned dowager whose daughter's debut had been less than spectacular.

Stanford liked Miss Marrenby. She was pretty and kind and easy to talk to. But the idea of marriage—to her or to anyone else—never crossed his mind. In fact, he found himself deeply annoyed whenever anyone hinted that he might be seriously contemplating the married state. He had decided to spend less time with Miss Marrenby in order to silence the gossips, and with this resolution in mind he moved away from her as soon as her attention was claimed by Lord Broome.

"The regent keeps his room uncomfortably warm, do you not agree, Lord Stanford?" said a woman's voice at his elbow, and he turned to look into the gold-flecked eyes of Lady Sophia Lowestoft.

Lady Sophia was a sophisticated woman of twenty-nine, widow of a much older man who had left her well provided for. She had not married again, but she never lacked for masculine companionship. The list of her lovers was small but select, and since she always maintained perfect discretion her standing in society was secure. She had returned to London only last week, and since then had signaled the young Viscount Stanford out for special attention. Before the regent's reception was over, Stanford had accepted an invitation to supper at her house in Mount Street the following evening.

He went with only one thing on his mind, and since Lady Sophia's mind was on a similar path they spent most of the evening in her bedroom. It had been a long time since Stanford had had a woman. Months of pain and then the exquisite anguish of learning to walk again had put any thoughts of sex far from his mind. But for the last month he had been feeling increasingly stronger, and he knew the reason for his growing tension and troubled dreams. He didn't know why it had taken him so long to do something about them. Or why, leaving Lady Sophia's house, he should feel so dissatisfied.

Lady Sophia had been more than pleased. Stanford had been a success with women ever since the age of sixteen, when one of the Dunstanburgh housemaids had seduced him. Women were a part of his life he rarely thought about. There always seemed to be a girl when he wanted one, and since he knew how to give pleasure as well as take it, he had always thought his relationships fair as well as satisfactory.

His encounter with Lady Sophia should have left him with a sense of well-being, the glow of enjoyment and fulfillment that he knew so well from other nights. But instead he was left with this feeling of vague dissatisfaction, of hunger for something lost. He knew it to be no fault of Lady Sophia's; it was in himself, but what caused it he did not know.

The reports Stanford received from the watch he had set on Gacé were disappointing. The duc kept no questionable company or clandestine appointments. He was not, apparently, faithful to his wife, a revelation which afforded Stanford an unreasonable sense of relief. He had the lady who enjoyed the duc's favors thoroughly investigated, and acquitted her of being a French spy.

Stanford sat at his desk one gray afternoon, the door firmly closed, revolving plans in his head. It was imperative that he isolate Gacé's contact; in order to expose him the duc must be apprehended in the act of passing secret information to a French agent. And the only way to do this, thought Stanford resignedly, was to give him some information to pass. With a sigh Stanford picked up some papers neatly piled on his desk. What secret information, useful but not vital, could he feed carelessly to the Duc de Gacé one chatty evening in his own library?

Those quiet chats with Stanford had already served to alarm the duc. As time went by and the tight security surrounding Wellington's plans refused to give way, Gacé became increasingly frustrated. Now, to add to his frustration, came the doubts that Stanford was planting about Napoleon's future. In fact, the duc was apprehensive that he might have chosen the wrong side.

His alliance with Napoleon was of relatively recent date. He had for seventeen years been the ardent royalist he appeared to be. A restoration of the monarchy had seemed to him the only way he could return to France and live out his life in the home of his ancestors. He had an immense esteem for tradition, and the royal family had always been linked to the fortunes of the de Vaudobins.

But gradually, as time went on, his hopes of a Bourbon restoration dwindled. Worse, it became clear that even if Louis XVIII returned as King of France he would not dare to alienate the new ruling class which had risen with Bonaparte. Aristocrats of the *ancien régime* might receive some compensation for their lost property, but there was very little chance of that property's being returned.

Compensation was not good enough for Matthieu de Vaudobin. He wanted the Château de Gacé, and nothing less. Then Napoleon defeated Austria and married an Austrian princess, linking himself dynastically to the Hapsburgs. It looked as if no one would ever depose him.

Soon afterward Gacé opened up correspondence with his numerous relatives and friends scattered all over Europe. In six months there wasn't a plot against Napoleon anywhere that he didn't know about. He began to share his information with the emperor.

His rationale was simple. If Louis couldn't return the Château de Gacé to him, Bonaparte could. His opportunities for growing in the emperor's esteem were greatly increased when Lord Liverpool's government came to power and Gacé was appointed to the Horse Guards. Once Napoleon defeated the Russians and the English, Gacé could return to France and name his reward.

Only now Napoleon's ultimate victory looked less sure than it had a year ago. The grand army had been destroyed in Russia, and Baron Stein had persuaded the czar to carry the war beyond Russian soil. A Russian-Prussian alliance was imminent, as Gacé knew from his source in Berlin. And Stanford had made him very uncomfortable about the possibility of Austria's joining the coalition. If Austria did come in, thought Gacé, Stanford was right about the German states.

From his calculations Gacé had come to two conclusions. One was that Austria's choice would be heavily influenced by what happened in Spain. It was essential that he break the secrecy surrounding Wellington's campaign plans. And two, he, Gacé, had better start looking for a way to secure his position with the royalists. If Napoleon did indeed fall, Gacé did not at all relish the idea of being exposed by the government in Paris as a spy.

Chapter 9

... return he cannot, nor
Continue where he is: to shift his being
Is to exchange one misery with another. . . .
—*Cymbeline*, I, v, 53-55

Stanford's liaison with Lady Sophia continued, but he found himself increasingly reluctant to visit her. For some reason he was in a foul mood, his temper precariously on edge. He dealt efficiently with the masses of paperwork that crossed his desk daily; and, exercising monumental tact and patience, he dealt with the Admiralty. The result was that the plans for Santander were running smoothly.

Menteith and Lord Bathurst were exceedingly pleased with the plans for the supply base, but impatient about their other problem. "I should have something to report shortly" was all Stanford would tell them, and, push him as they might, they could get no more out of him.

In fact, with his usual ruthless efficiency, he had given Gacé some of the details of the alliance talks presently being conducted between England and Sweden. He then notified the two men he had following Gacé to be especially alert and to report immediately any unusual contact the duc might make.

This game he was playing with Gacé must be preying on his nerves, Stanford decided one rainy evening while dining at White's with Charles Doune and some friends.

He was in no mood for company; he was black-tempered and edgy, and the damp made his leg ache.

"The only company I am fit for this evening is my own," he excused himself to his party. "I think I'll return to Berkeley Square."

"Where are Nanda and Gacé tonight?" Charles Doune asked.

"They were dining with Lord Liverpool, I believe," Stanford answered.

But when he returned to Gacé House at about eleven o'clock it was to find Nanda in the drawing room reading a book. He stood in the doorway for a moment watching her. She wore an evening gown of dusty-rose crepe that brought out the warmth of her skin. Her dark hair was dressed simply in a shining chignon at the nape of her long, graceful neck. He had made no sound, but after a moment she looked around and saw him. Her eyebrows arched in surprise. "What are you doing home at this hour?"

He advanced a few steps into the room. "I might ask you the same question."

"Ginny had a toothache this afternoon, and after the ordeal of a trip to the dentist, I felt the need for a little quiet. Matthieu was perfectly happy to go to Lord Liverpool's by himself.

"Poor Ginny."

"Poor Ginny, indeed!" she retorted, a glint of amusement in her dark eyes. "Poor me, you mean. Let me tell you, my lord, there is nothing worse than taking a reluctant child to the dentist. They recover from the experience much more readily than the exhausted parent."

He felt his lips move in the expected smile. He heard her say in her rich, slightly husky voice, "And what are you doing home so early? I thought you were dining with Charles."

His voice seemed to come from far away. "Like you, I felt the need of some quiet." He felt very strange, as if his skin had disappeared and all his nerves were exposed and vibrating to the presence of the woman seated so gracefully before the fire. His eyes, as he looked at her, were such a dense blue they seemed opaque.

Nanda sensed there was something the matter with him, and for a moment she was at a loss. Then, seeing the grim set of his mouth, she thought she understood. His leg was bothering him and, being Adam, he hated to admit it. A feeling of tenderness, such as she felt for Marc when he gallantly took on a task too difficult for his four-year-old's dexterity, flooded her. "Then I won't keep you here talking," she said gently. "Goodnight, Adam."

It took a moment for her words to penetrate his brain. Her eyes on his face were enormous and full of light. "Goodnight," she said, and smiled. The smile shattered him. With great difficulty he controlled his breathing. He realized he was expected to go, and with a harsh "Goodnight" he left the room and walked mechanically up the stairs to the privacy of his room.

He opened the curtains and stood for a long time at the window, looking down at the rain pooling under the lamps on the street, his face white as a bleached bone. He understood now why Lady Sophia had not interested him. It was Nanda he wanted. His breathing was painful. Nanda. He thought of her eyes, her mouth, her body.

Christ, he thought. I can't stay in this house. Impossible to see her every day, to be easy and friendly; not to let her know.

He had thought he was safe. He had seen through Gacé's game; he was not a fish to be caught by the lure of Gacé's wife.

But, little by little, she had invaded his mind and his soul until he stood here now aching for what he could not have. And he knew that what he felt was not a transient desire. He was familiar with them, and this was different. This was not just a lovely woman he wanted in his bed; this was Nanda. Nanda, whose clear, thinking mind was able to match his own; Nanda, whose fidelity and courage had seen her through the barren wastes of a loveless marriage; Nanda, whose loving spirit was ready to sacrifice itself for the welfare of two children; Nanda, whose face and body were the most beautiful things he had ever seen. I must get away, he thought. But I can't. Because of Gacé.

Because of Gacé, and the threat he posed, he must stay here. He must hide his love and his desire. He must pretend that nothing had happened. And, on the surface, nothing had.

The Duc de Gacé, unaware of the suspicions harbored against him by his houseguest, was engaged in reconsidering his own position. If Napoleon were victorious, he had no doubt that a great reward awaited him in Paris. But if Napoleon should fall . . .

For years Gacé had schemed for just that to happen: the fall of the upstart Bonaparte and the restoration of the Bourbons. It was supremely ironic, he thought as he sat cogitating in the library at Gacé House one morning, his mail on the desk in front of him, that now, when he had forsaken the monarchy and gone over to his enemy, it looked as if the invincible Bonaparte might be taken after all.

Gacé's hopes still lay with Napoleon. It was in the duc's interests to see the emperor triumphant—and grateful. But only a fool, Gacé decided, would fail to plan for all contingencies. Most important, at the moment, was to arrange for a place he could safely retreat to in case matters became uncomfortable for him in England. Gacé had no desire to hang as a spy.

He read through his mail slowly, a slight frown between his elegant eyebrows. The last letter was from a cousin of his in Baden, and Gacé put it down with a sudden decisive motion. Baden, he decided, was the very place. The duc had resided in Baden for years after fleeing from France. Baden was where Ginny had been born and where his first wife was buried. In fact, Gacé owned an estate on the east bank of the Rhine, Niederwald Castle, which had been run for him by a steward for the last six years.

Politically, Baden was part of the Confederation of the Rhine and loyal to Napoleon. In fact, Grand Duke Carl was married to Stephanie de Beauharnais, Napoleon's stepdaughter. But Gacé knew that Stanford had been correct in his assessment of the loyalty of the Rhenish Confederation: the moment it looked as if Napoleon might fall, Baden, Bavaria, and their sister states would desert him.

With a sardonic smile playing around his lips, Gacé reflected that Baden was in much the same position as he was himself: collaborating with both sides and determined to be on the winning end. If things became worrisome here, Baden was clearly the best place to remove to. He would put some distance between himself and England. The Germans would hardly be likely to point an accusing finger at him; they were all tarnished with the same brush he was. And if the English tried to make trouble for him, he had Nanda, the sister of the Earl of Menteith, to hold over them. She would come with him, he thought. He had the children.

Nanda's future was something Stanford was not allowing himself to think about. Inevitably she would be seriously affected by Gacé's exposure. As of yet, however, Stanford had nothing to prove Gacé's complicity but his own suspicions. Once he was sure, then he could worry about how to handle it. The most important thing at the moment was to satisfy himself that Gacé was in fact the traitor he sought.

Since the night he had come home early and found her in the drawing room he had seen very little of Nanda. When they did meet his manner was courteous and impersonal, a return of his behavior when he had first come to Berkeley Square. On the rare occasions when he was alone with her for a few moments she had such a strong impression of his reserve that the barrier between them seemed almost physical. On one occasion she had asked him hesitantly, "Have I offended you in any way, Adam?"

They were dining in before going to a reception, and Stanford had come down deliberately late to avoid being alone with her, but Gacé was later still. "Of course you haven't offended me," he answered. "Why should you think that?"

She smiled a little. "Only that you have been rather distant lately. I thought perhaps you were avoiding me."

He was not smiling. He looked up slowly and met her gaze, his own level. "I beg your pardon for my rudeness. I have only been rather busy and consequently somewhat preoccupied."

The luminous brown eyes remained fixed on his face for a moment. Then, as she was about to answer, Gacé came into the room. Stanford turned to him, hoping the relief he felt did not show in his face. As soon as they reached the reception he separated from them and Nanda saw him circulating among the company and then standing talking for a long time with Lord Bathurst, the war minister. He looked like a man who was trying to ignore a raging headache.

Chapter 10

There cannot be a pinch in death
More sharp than this is.

—*Cymbeline*, I, i, 130-31

Lady Castlereagh gave her first reception on February 22, and many people who had been in the country returned to town to attend. Lady Castlereagh's rooms were filled with the bluest blood and the loveliest women in London, and prominent among the guests were the Duc de Gacé and his beautiful wife.

Nanda had taken special pains with her appearance, and the result was stunning. She wore a new gown of pale champagne crepe cut in a deep décolleté in front to show off a string of beautiful matched pearls, scarcely more luminous than her skin. She was all pale cream; the only colors about her were her enormous, black-fringed eyes and the rich darkness of her shining hair.

Gacé was pleased with her. There was a look in his eyes that she recognized, and she felt his hand resting caressingly on her bare skin as he helped her with her cloak. He took her arm and bent to say something to her in his light, careful voice. With an effort she gazed serenely up at him, her nerves uncomfortably on edge.

Adam Todd was standing at the far side of the room watching the duc and duchesse when he was joined by Lady Sophia Lowestoft. "They make an elegant couple, do they not?" she said shrewdly, following his gaze. His profile was rigidly calm, the mask of a mind that was far from peaceful. His eyes remained a moment longer on the tall, fair aristocrat and the slender, dark-haired girl, then he turned to her.

"How have you been, Sophia?" he asked evenly.

"Lonely," she answered softly, her eyes going once more to the Duchesse de Gacé. Then she put her hand on his arm and said softly, "When are you coming to visit me, Adam?"

He stared at her a minute, his face somber. "When do you want me?" he said finally.

"Tonight? You could escort me home."

There was a pause, then he smiled at her, his blue eyes hard. "Why not?" he answered lightly.

"Why not indeed?" she responded, her golden eyes hazy with expectation.

It was early morning when Stanford returned to Gacé House. He did not look like a man returning from a night of pleasure. He let himself in and went quietly up the stairs, the candle steady in his hand. As he reached his bedroom a door opened down the hall and Gacé, wearing a velvet dressing gown, came out. He turned in surprise when he saw Stanford's light, then smiled. "Sleep well, Stanford," he said, his light voice warm with amusement. "Goodnight."

"Goodnight, Gacé," Stanford answered mechanically and, opening the door, entered his bedroom. He stood for a long time in front of the closed door, his face stark in the moonlight from the window. Gacé had been coming out of her room.

Stanford drew a deep, shuddering breath, then another. He swore suddenly as the candle tumbled from his hand to the floor. He looked without comprehension at the broken stick in his hand and at the extinguished candle on the floor. Slowly he bent, picked it up and laid it on a table in the moonlight. He had snapped the china candlestick in his hand. The violence he felt within himself was terrible. With sudden decision he turned, left the room, and went back down the stairs. He didn't know where he was going. He only knew he had to get out of this house.

For the next few days Stanford barely showed his face at Berkeley Square. The only person in the family who appeared to be in good spirits was the duc. Nanda had a nagging headache which accounted, she told herself, for her continuing feeling of depression. Ginny was unaccountably testy, and Marc broke a window playing cricket in the garden. Nanda was expecting his nurse to return in three days' time and prayed she wouldn't murder him before Miss Fergus arrived to take charge of the nursery once again.

It was Marc, however, who precipitated the biggest crisis Nanda had yet had to face in her young life. She was tucking him into bed one cold, blowy evening when his small, strong arms reached up to clutch around her neck. "Mama, I want to whisper," he said urgently.

Obediently she inclined her head. "What is it, darling?"

"I wish Adam were my papa," he said, then looked at her with frightened and defiant eyes.

There was a moment's silence, then she said carefully, "You mustn't say that, Marc. Adam can't be your papa; you already have a papa. But Adam can be your friend, and that is a very good thing."

"I guess so," the little boy said reluctantly. "I love Adam, Mama."

"I know, darling," she said gently. "Go to sleep now."

"All right." As she reached the door he sat up again. "And I love you, Mama."

She laughed shakily. "I know, Marc. I love you too. Now go to sleep, darling."

Marc lay down again and Nanda went calmly down the stairs to the drawing room. Gacé had been suddenly called away to visit an old friend, and Nanda had decided to stay home.

She sat in front of the fire and stared into it, her mind haunted by Marc's words. "I wish Adam were my papa," he had said. And, unbidden, the response had leaped in her heart. "So do I."

Her mouth was severe with pain as she stared into the flames, determined to face her private terrors. She thought first of Gacé. She had been seventeen years old when she had met Matthieu. She had misread him. She had not seen the egotism that lay under his charm and his sensitive face. He lived in the isolated desert of his pride: his name, his lineage, this was all that mattered to him.

A servant came in to build the fire, and she told him the staff could retire for the night. She leaned back in her chair and closed her eyes. With characteristic honesty, she admitted to herself that if she had been deceived, then so had Matthieu. He had married a girl from one of the best families in the country; a girl, moreover, twenty years younger than he. He had not asked much; he simply wanted her to adore him, to think everything he did was perfect. And she had. He had had no reason to believe she would change. It was only when he realized that she had a mind of her own, and a moral sense that stood in judgment on him and on his standards, that he had taken alarm.

They had come to a truce, and the current of their marriage had run relatively smoothly during the past several years. A number of things helped in facilitating this calm. One was the fact that they resided in Great Britain, where Gacé was the outsider and Nanda and her family the standard. Nanda's determination to be as happy as possible was another aid, as was her extraordinary beauty. Gacé's pride was flattered by knowing his wife to be the most desirable woman in London. And, even in the bitterest year of their marriage, she had always had the power to stir his senses.

Very little had changed in her life of late, she thought, sitting before the fire on this cold, windy March night. But the resignation was gone. Life with Matthieu was no longer tolerable for her, and until tonight she had not known why.

"I wish Adam were my papa."

It was Adam Todd who had brought this discontent to her. Unconsciously she had been comparing him: to Matthieu, to all the other men she knew. By contrast they were shadows, substanceless and vague. She knew now why none of the men who had paid court to her in the past had interested her.

She sat on late into the night until the fire dimmed and the candles burned down. At about four in the morning the drawing-room door opened and Stanford stood on the threshold. "What are you doing sitting alone here at this hour?" His voice was rough with concern as he took in the dim room and her still figure.

She said nothing, and after a moment's hesitation he came into the room. She sat in a narrow wing chair, her head leaned against the dark wine-colored back. Her face was pure as a cameo against the velvet. Slowly she fixed her eyes on him. "You look tired," she said.

His blue eyes were steady on her face. What he saw there caused the breath, silently, to leave his body. "That is your fault," he said finally.

He saw the surprise on her face. "I couldn't bear to be near you," he said levelly, but she could see that he was controlling his breath. "I love you too much." Then, as she continued to look at him in wonder, he held out his hands. "Come here."

Very slowly she rose, crossed the room, and stood before him, her head tipped back to look into his face. "Nanda," he said. His eyes were black, not blue. He bent his head and began to kiss her.

She had not expected it. He could sense the surprise in her slender, unresisting body. He didn't want to frighten her, but the feel of her between his hands, the softness of her mouth under his, were too much for the pent-up desire of weeks. He pulled her to him with hard strength, his lips urgent and demanding on hers.

A slight shudder shook her, then, slowly, of her own volition, her arms came up to circle his neck. Her body arched to press against his, her lips opened, and she returned his kiss.

They stood thus for a long minute, locked together in mutual passion. Then Stanford, conscious only of his own driving need, began to move her toward the sofa.

Nanda's eyes were closed. He was surprisingly strong; her feet were off the ground. They reached the sofa and, feeling the surrender in her mouth, he bent to pick her up.

A log cracked loudly on the dying fire and the flames shot up for a minute, then died down again. Nanda jumped and stiffened in his arms. It took him a minute to realize she was pushing him away. With a tremendous effort of will he released her. She backed away toward the door.

"No," she said breathlessly.

"Why?" His voice was harsh; he felt sure she could hear the hammering of his heart.

Her eyes were great pools of black in her warmly tinted face. Her hair had loosened and hung in a silky mass on her shoulders. "It is too late," she said shakily. "I have been sitting here all night thinking of how much I love you. But it is too late."

"Where is Gacé?"

"It doesn't matter. Adam, please leave this house. Go away from me."

He had himself under control now, but his breathing was still uneven. A pulse began to beat in his temple. "I can't," he said. He was deathly pale.

She hesitated a moment, as if she would throw herself once more in his arms, then turned and ran to the door. He heard her feet on the staircase. He stood looking after her, his face for once unguarded. He understood her terror, her bitter fear of destroying what for five years she had so carefully nurtured. But "I love you," she had said. He would do anything in the world for her, he thought. Except give her up.

Chapter 11

To your protection I commend me, gods.
From fairies and the tempters of the night
Guard me, beseech ye!

—*Cymbeline*, II, ii, 8-10

For the rest of that night and for the next few days
Nanda fought a bitter battle with herself. With the honesty
that was an integral part of her nature she faced the
truth of her emotions: she loved Adam Todd. She had
crossed over the river of friendship and stood now on a
foreign shore where the light was blinding and the hunger
burning. That wild desire she had felt—to know, to
give, to be given to—could not be denied. It existed, and
each day it grew stronger. But the even more painful
truth she forced herself to acknowledge was the conclusion
that any relationship between them was impossible.

It was a decision she made with characteristic courage.
For five years Nanda had lived with the knowledge that
her own interests were, and had to be, secondary to
those of her children. For the sake of those children she
must remain married to their father. An affair with Stanford
was always a possibility, and such was Nanda's anguish
that she considered it. So long as they were
discreet, her world, and perhaps even her husband,
would turn a blind eye. But Nanda had been raised in a
warm, loving, but strict Scottish family. What she
thought was right did not always coincide with the prevailing
social mores. Adultery, she had no doubt at all,
was wrong.

Besides, she did not want a transient affair with Adam

78

Todd. She wanted permanence. And permanence she could not have.

What he wanted she did not know. He had said he loved her. Certainly he desired her. It was only natural that he should, she thought, considering their propinquity over the past few months. She had strong suspicions that he would forget all about her once he returned to the Peninsula. She, unfortunately, would never forget him.

She had tried, once again, to convince him to leave Berkeley Square, but with a notable lack of success. He had looked at her with eyes that made her shiver, and refused to go. And as long as he remained where she was forced to see him and to hear his voice, she knew she was not safe. She could not trust her own heart. In desperation she wrote a letter to her brother Robert.

Lord Menteith was surprised to get Nanda's note requesting him to call on her the next morning and to say nothing to anyone about the visit. He was mystified, slightly worried, and presented himself promptly the following morning at ten o'clock.

"Is there anything wrong, Nan?" he asked, after he had been shown into the morning parlor by the butler to find his sister making tea.

She looked up from the teapot to meet her brother's kind, concerned eyes. "No," she said.

"I'm glad to hear it," he answered, accepting a cup from her. "Children all right?"

"Oh, yes. Fergie finally returned to us, and life has been considerably calmer."

"I'm glad to hear it," he responded courteously. "Gacé is fine, I know, as I see him virtually every day. How are you?"

"Me? Oh I'm all right, Robert."

He cocked a skeptical eyebrow at her. "You don't look all right. You're too thin, for one thing, and there are shadows under those famous eyes." He put his cup down. "What's wrong, Nannie?" he said gently. "You wanted to see me for *some* reason."

The gentleness in his voice and the use of her nursery name brought tears welling to her eyes. Before they could overflow, however, she had herself in hand and answered in a reasonably steady voice. "I wanted to see you, Robert, to ask if there was any way you could get Lord Stanford transferred away from the Horse Guards."

For a moment he looked at her in stunned silence. "Get Stanford transferred?" he repeated in a bewildered voice. "But why?"

She did not answer, but bright color burned in her cheeks. Bravely, she met his eyes.

"Oh my God," he said. "What's happened?"

"Nothing, Robert," she said steadily. "And nothing will happen, if you can get him away from this house."

"Can't you ask him to leave yourself?"

"I have." The color in her cheeks burned even brighter. "He won't go."

Looking at her, Menteith had a feeling that he was out of his depth. "I think, Nanda, you had better tell me exactly what this is all about."

"It is very simple, Robert," she said wearily. "I am in love with Adam Todd, but there is nothing I can do about it. There is nothing I intend to do about it. However, I do not enjoy being tortured"—for a moment her level voice quivered—"by his continual presence in my house."

"And Stanford?"

"He won't leave. I believe he still has . . . hopes."

"Oh my God," he repeated, his hand running through his hair in a characteristic gesture.

"Precisely. You can imagine the depths of my own feelings since I found it necessary to confide in you."

Lord Menteith's honest brown eyes were unusually bleak as he looked at his young sister. "That damned marriage," he said. "I knew it was a mistake and I let you go through with it."

She reached out and took his hand. "Please don't blame yourself, Robert. It was no one's mistake but my own. And, really, I can't even say I'm sorry I made it."

He looked at the lovely, earnest face looking so pleadingly at him, raised her hand to his lips briefly, and said, "What do you mean, you're not sorry you married Gacé? Don't try to tell me your life has been a pleasure."

"No, but how can I regret the change in Ginny? Or be sorry I had Marc?"

"I know what you are saying, Nanda, but I can't bear to see you sacrifice your whole life because of two children. Surely there is some way out. We would all support you if you separated from Gacé."

"Robert, don't you think I've been through this hundreds of times in my own head? Possibly, because of family power, I might win custody of Marc. But Ginny? I haven't a chance of getting Ginny."

"But would Gacé want to keep her?"

"Keep her, his daughter with royal blood in her veins? Of course he would keep her. And marry her, no doubt, into some royal Continental family where she would be miserable. But," and her eyes lit with determination, "he won't do that if I am around to stop him. And I plan to be around, Robert. So, really, there is nothing else to say."

He looked at her, his own face somber. "Nanda, for five years you have tried to fool us all into believing you were happy. You fooled no one, but you tried. This feeling you have for Stanford must be strong indeed to force you to reveal yourself like this."

Now she refused to meet his eyes. "As you say."

He took a deep breath. "Nan, I can't get him transferred from the Horse Guards."

"Why not?"

"The work he is involved in is too important. It can't be turned over to anyone else."

"Work involving the coming campaign?"

He hesitated. "Yes."

"But Robert," she said reasonably, "if Lord Stanford had not been available because of his wound, someone else would have done it. Don't tell me there is no one else at the Horse Guards capable of organizing a campaign."

"No one half as efficient as Stanford," he replied truthfully.

Her brown eyes narrowed with sudden comprehension. "There is more to it than the campaign, isn't there?" she said shrewdly.

He looked at her in exasperation. "Of course not, Nanda. What are you talking about?"

"I don't know," she answered slowly. "But there's something you're not telling me, Robert. That much I do understand."

His mouth tightened. "Possibly. But if I don't tell you, Nan, it's for a dashed good reason."

She nodded. "I see. And you cannot transfer him?"

"No. But I can invite him to stay with me."

The shadows under her eyes looked suddenly bluer. "Don't waste your time, Robert. He won't accept."

"When I get through with him he will," Menteith answered grimly.

"No!" it was a cry of pure distress. "Robert, I won't be able to bear it if you tell him I've talked to you."

"But Nanda—"

"No!" Her eyes blazed at him. "I spoke to you in deepest confidence, and if you betray me, Robert, I shall never speak to you again."

He looked at her angry face and, reluctantly, acquiesced. "All right, Nanda, I'll hold my tongue. But Stanford's assignment should be concluding soon. As soon as it does, I'll see him sent packing." He rose and went to kiss her warm cheek. "Another month or two, my dear, and he'll be gone."

She saw him to the door and then returned to the morning parlor. Another month or two, she thought, as she stood regarding the half-filled teacups. Another month or two of hell. However was she to get through it?

Gacé had received word from his cousin at the court of Frederick William in Berlin that Prussia and Russia had signed a treaty of alliance on February 27. Bernadotte of Sweden was on the point of concluding a treaty with England. The coalition opposing Napoleon was beginning to re-form.

On the other hand, as Gacé knew, Austria had not yet moved. Napoleon was confident. He had a large new army. And he felt his marriage to an Austrian princess had secured Austria to him as an ally. In a like manner Napoleon had taken care to marry members of his family to the princely rulers of Germany.

Gacé placed no confidence at all in this kind of alliance. The Emperor Francis would like nothing more than to see his son-in-law toppled and European leadership restored to Austria. Nor would the German princes' ancient connections with the Hapsburgs and the Romanovs be easily outweighed by a few marriages to the upstart Bonapartes.

Gacé, whatever his morals, had an excellent brain and an astute sense of politics. Austria, he knew, was not committing herself because of Russia. Metternich knew well that Austria was poorly armed and financially depleted, and to join the alliance now would be to become dependent on Russia. Austria's plan was to restore the balance of European power, not to move it from France to Russia. Austria would stay neutral and play a waiting game.

Napoleon's future security depended upon a smashing victory in Spain. This was the conclusion Gacé came to. And it was very much in Gacé's interest to see Napoleon triumphant. His own position, otherwise, would be extremely equivocal.

To Gacé's great relief, the young Viscount Stanford was finally showing signs of confiding in him. Within a few weeks he hoped to have Wellington's plans to send on to Paris.

Chapter 12

Had I this cheek
To bathe my lips upon; this hand, whose touch,
Whose every touch, would force the feeler's soul
To the oath of loyalty; this object, which
Takes prisoner the wild motion of mine eye,
Fixing it only here ...

—*Cymbeline*, I, vi, 99-104

Jem Martin stood inside Fawley's Bookshop in Piccadilly, his gaze intent on a copy of *Childe Harold*. In the next aisle, separated from him by only a row of bookcases, was Matthieu de Vaudobin, Duc de Gacé. Martin had followed Gacé to this bookstore once before and was interested to notice that on both occasions Gacé had met the same man.

The tall aristocrat and the small, dark Frenchman—Martin had heard his accent the last time, when he had purchased a book—stood very close to each other, apparently absorbed in the row of books before them. They spoke together in low tones and, though Martin's straining ears did manage to catch a phrase or two, it was only to discover that they spoke in French, a language he did not understand. They left the store separately, but Martin observed a phenomenon he had been told to look for.

"You were right, Mr. Devon," he told Stanford several hours later at the Green Oak. "When the Frenchie left he was carrying the book the duc had been holding."

A light glimmered deep in Stanford's blue eyes. "I think at last we're getting somewhere, Jem."

"Yes sir," Jem replied doubtfully.

Stanford smiled briefly. "We are, I assure you. Now, Jem, the next time the duc meets this gentleman in the bookshop I want you to follow the Frenchman."

"Leave the duc, do you mean?"

"Precisely. Leave the duc and follow the Frenchman. I want to know where he goes. I suspect he will head for the coast, and if he does it is very important that you discover whom he makes contact with. Do you understand me?"

Jem's mouth looked grim. "Aye, Mr. Devon, well enough. Spies, are they?"

"Possibly."

"Well, you need have no fear, sir. I'll track that Frenchie or my name ain't Jem Martin."

"Thank you, Jem." Stanford rose from behind the scarred table and leaned slightly toward the nondescript man sitting across from him. "But remember, everything you do must be held in strictest secrecy. You will report only to me."

Jem looked into the steely blue of Stanford's eyes and nodded vigorously. "Of course," he said. "Of course, Mr. Devon."

At Berkeley Square, Nanda had found means to avoid being alone with Stanford. On every possible occasion when he might be likely to find her solitary during the day she had one of the children with her. And in the evenings she went out. There was scarcely a dinner party that lacked her presence. She went often to the opera and the theater, and several hostesses were delighted indeed to have the unexpected honor of her presence at their balls.

Stanford, who knew perfectly well what she was doing, watched her from a distance and bided his time. He, too, was to be seen at numerous social affairs, and the ton was interested to note that his liaison with Lady Sophia Lowestoft seemed to have come to an end.

In fact, breaking off with Lady Sophia had been a trifle awkward. She was the one who had called a halt to all her previous affairs, and being given her dismissal by a lover was a totally new and unpleasant experience for her. She had been suspicious and had asked a great many questions. Stanford, fearful she would stumble on the truth, said hastily that he was thinking of getting married and thought he would have a better chance of being accepted if he were—ah—unencumbered.

Lady Sophia's eyes had turned very gold. "Married, my lord. To whom? The Marrenby girl?"

"That, Sophia, is none of your affair," he had replied pleasantly. And he had left with a slightly guilty feeling of having behaved not quite fairly to Miss Marrenby.

He went out of his way at the parties he attended to demonstrate to the social world his unattached heart. He took care never to slight Miss Marrenby, but he took care also not to devote himself to her, or to raise false hopes. He knew, from a certain warmth in her eyes, that she was not indifferent to him, and to use her as a disguise for his real feelings would be unpardonable. If she had been interested only in his money and his position he would not have hesitated to indulge her with a flirtation. But whatever his attraction for her mother, Elizabeth, he thought, liked him for himself. So he treated her gently.

Nanda was aware of his watching eyes. Try as she might to avoid him, he seemed to be ubiquitous. He had only to enter a room for her to be instantly aware of his presence. She had no need to turn around; she felt him there, watching her with those intense blue eyes. Her nerves became tauter and tauter, until she felt like a too tightly strung bow, ready to snap at the slightest pressure.

He found her alone one evening in the saloon at Gacé House. She was dressed for the opera in a fawn-colored silk gown of elegant cut, her hair dressed high and caught with rubies. Rubies shone too in her ears and on her breast. She whirled around when he came in, her breath catching in her throat. "I thought you were going to your aunt's," she said, her voice harsh in her own ears.

He was dressed for the evening in a perfectly fitting black coat and snowy-white waistcoat, shirt, and cravat. "I am. I'm on my way," he answered briefly.

She said nothing, only stood quite still, looking at him, her eyes full of pain and longing. The moment seemed to stretch out interminably, then she whispered, "Go away. Can't you see you are wearing me out?"

The despair in her voice tore at his vitals, but he answered steadily, "And what do you think you are doing to me?" She turned her head, but he said again, sharply, "Look at me, Nanda. I love you. Do you think I enjoy this cat-and-mouse game we are playing any more than you do?"

Her voice was muffled. "Then why won't you go away?"

"Because I can't." Bitter anger sounded in his voice, and she raised her eyes once more to his face. "You don't believe me, do you?" he said. "You don't believe I love you."

"Oh, Adam." She gestured helplessly. "Don't you understand that, whatever we may feel, there is no future for us? If I had met you five years ago, when I was unattached—"

Stanford cut in across her voice. "It is not quite as easy as that, Nanda. Perhaps five years ago I would have loved you, but not the way I feel about you today." He came across the three steps that separated them and stood quietly before her. "You see, my darling," he said gently, "it is Gacé's wife that I love."

For a moment she stopped breathing, then, unconsciously, her hand went out toward him. At her touch something as elemental as lightning seemed to flash between them, and he moved to pull her into his arms.

There was the sound of a step outside the door, and in a moment Gacé was in the room. "Stanford," he said, a note of surprise in his careful voice. "I thought you were dining at the Crosbys'."

"I am. I just stopped in to have a word with her grace." To her ears Stanford's voice sounded almost normal, a far cry from the bitter "Hell!" that had sounded in her ears at Gacé's approach. With an effort she turned to smile hesitantly at him, a formal farewell to satisfy the curious eyes of her husband.

She was distracted all evening. She scarcely heard a note of the opera and stared into space at the intermissions unconscious of the smiles of friends that were directed toward her as she sat between the red, festooned curtains of their opera box. As the evening progressed a fierce and painful knowledge grew within her heart.

Again and again she heard his words: ". . . it is Gacé's wife I love." He understood. Like her he did not regret the past, the difficult, painful years when she had fought for the future of her children. For them she had learned to be sagacious and smiling, tactful and dignified, watchful and ruthless. The fierce and passionate heart that beat within her today would have been unrecognizable to the sweetly gentle girl she had been at eighteen. Everything that was strong about her had come out of those five years.

It was Gacé's wife he loved. And she loved him; with an aching need that tore at her vitals and rent her heart, she loved him. This new knowledge only made more agonizing the lesson she had already learned: any relationship between them was impossible.

Several times Gacé looked at her, a slight frown between his fair brows. He had to repeat himself almost every time he addressed her. Finally, "Are you all right, Nanda?" he asked. "Would you like to go home?"

"No!" she shook her head a little and laughed apologetically. "I am sorry to be such poor company, Matthieu. I am all right, really."

"If you are sure . . ."

"I am."

At that point the music started up again and she turned to the stage in obvious relief.

She didn't want time to be alone. To think. It only made things worse.

And still Stanford watched her. He watched her with pity, but also with a grim realization that he could not allow her to have things her way. Perhaps if he hadn't known about Gacé's treachery, he would have respected her loyalty and left her alone. Perhaps.

He had known perfectly well that she had discounted his feelings. She had lived for five years with a man who found her desirable but who did not love her. She was constantly surrounded by men whose eyes gleamed with controlled passion when they danced or spoke with her. It was not at all surprising that she should put him in that category.

It had made him angry. He had sought in vain for a chance to speak to her, to make her see the truth of his love, but she had protected herself too well. It had taken him weeks to find an opportunity, and then his time had been all too brief.

But it had been enough. He knew, as he watched her in the days following their encounter, that he had been successful. He loved her, and now she knew that he loved her. He knew also that she was only waiting for the day when he would leave.

Stanford had no intention of going, nor was he content to leave matters so unfulfilled between them. He wanted a commitment from her, and he knew of only one way to get that.

Nanda de Vaudobin was a woman rare in her class and age, a woman to whom the act of sex mattered. It was more than a momentary pleasure, to be lightly given and as lightly forgotten. It meant, for her, what Stanford wanted: a commitment, a promise not lightly given and not to be forgotten.

Because he loved her he understood this. At the moment her formidable conscience stood between them, but Stanford was determined to win this particular struggle. And Stanford, when he set his mind on something, could be ruthless. It was this quality of ruthlessness, honed by years of war, that had so disconcerted his father upon his return. Now he watched Nanda and he waited. It was only a question of opportunity.

Chapter 13

Swift, swift, you dragons of the night, that dawning
May bare the raven's eye! I lodge in fear. . . .
—*Cymbeline*, II, ii, 48-49

Charles Doune was worried about his sister. She looked as if she had lost weight, and her brilliant eyes were too large for her pale face. He decided, since he had gotten no satisfaction from Nanda, to take the matter up with his eldest brother.

He went to see Menteith at the Horse Guards one afternoon after he had left White's. The earl had been at a meeting, and when he came to greet his brother there was such a look of satisfaction on his face that Charles' eyebrows rose.

"You look like a cat who has just finished a saucer of cream, Rob," he remarked amiably.

Menteith laughed. "Not quite, Charles, but I am pleased. The organization for the coming campaign is going very well indeed. Largely due, I might add, to Lord Stanford. I don't know how the man did it, but he has actually won willing cooperation from the navy."

Charles laughed. "A remarkable achievement."

"It is!" Menteith retorted. "If only you knew the trouble I have had in the past. But now it seems as if the admirals are eating out of our hands. I call it a most remarkable achievement indeed."

"It seems it was a good day's work when you brought Stanford into the department. All too often the men who are brilliant in the field are useless when it comes to administration. Apparently that is not true in his case."

"No," Menteith agreed, "it is most certainly not true in his case. He combines the virtue of a comprehensive grasp of major principles with an attention to detail that is formidable at the least."

"In short, he understands both the ends and the means."

"Exactly." Menteith smiled ruefully, "We have people in the department who are quite good at one or the other, but very few who can be trusted with both."

"Will he be rejoining the army, then, or do you plan to keep him here?"

Menteith's face suddenly became wooden. "His leg, as you know, Charles, is still not completely healed. When it is, I suspect Lord Stanford will return to the Peninsula. Lord Wellington certainly wishes him to do so."

Charles looked with interest at his brother's face. "I see," he said with no expression in his voice. "What I really came to see you about, Robert," he said, seemingly changing the subject, "is Nanda."

"Nanda!" Menteith, if anything, looked more wooden than ever.

"Yes, Nanda. Our sister. Our only sister." Charles' eyes were suddenly shrewd.

"What about Nanda?" said Menteith.

"I don't like the way she has been looking lately."

"Looking?"

"Dammit, Robert, stop repeating everything I say. Yes, looking! As if, as if something tragic had happened to her."

"Trag—" Menteith started to repeat, then stopped himself. "Dash it all, Charles, I don't know what you are talking about."

"Oh, you don't." Charles leaned forward, a frown on his dark, handsome face. "Then you mustn't have seen her lately. She hardly hears a word one says. She's thin and pale and looks as if she'll snap in two any minute. Is it something to do with Gacé?"

"Gacé?" said Menteith.

Charles brought his hand down on Menteith's desk. "Stop playing games with me, Robert!"

"Why should you think Nanda's appearance has something to do with Gacé?"

"Because he has a perfect genius for making her unhappy. His very presence is a blight."

Menteith carefully moved some papers around on his desk. With his eyes studiously avoiding Charles' he said, "It has been so for years. Why, now, should Nanda suddenly be so disturbed by him?"

"I don't know," Charles answered restlessly. "But I know she is disturbed, more so than I've ever seen her to be. I wish you will tell me if there's something I can do for her."

Menteith ran his hand through his thick, straight hair. "There is nothing we can do, Charles, either of us, to help Nanda now. Except, perhaps, to leave her alone."

"There is something wrong," Charles said slowly. "I knew it."

"Yes, there is something wrong. But there is nothing either of us can do about it, Charles." Menteith would not meet his eyes.

"Is it the children?"

"No."

"Then what?"

"I can't tell you, Charles," Menteith repeated patiently. "Believe me when I say there is nothing we can do. And things will get better presently."

There was a pause, then Charles said, a challenge in his eyes, "When Stanford returns to the army?"

Menteith's eyes looked up to meet the dark gaze of his younger brother. There was a tense silence, then Menteith said quietly, "You and Nanda were always very close."

"Yes. That is probably why she has been avoiding me lately."

"There is nothing between them, Charles."

"Except that Nanda loves him."

Menteith's silence was his answer.

Wearily, Charles got to his feet. "Why don't you send the fellow away, Robert?"

"I can't. And if I could, I doubt if he'd go."

"I suppose not."

Both men stared intently at Charles' driving gloves, lying on the edge of the desk. Then Menteith said, as if the words were wrenched out of him, "Do you think he loves her, Charles?"

Charles' smile was not pleasant. "Have you ever seen the poor devil's eyes when he looks at her? They don't make many like Stanford, Robert, but I fear he is doomed to failure, another of Nanda's sacrifices on the altar of her wretched marriage. It would give me a good deal of satisfaction to see Gacé rotting in hell," he said viciously. He picked up his driving gloves and went to the door, his handsome face dark with anger.

Menteith waited until his hand was on the door. "I don't know about that, Charles," he said then, softly.

Charles' hand dropped. "What don't you know, Rob?"

"If Stanford is doomed to failure."

Surprise flared in Charles Doune's brown eyes. For a long minute the two brothers looked at each other, then Charles drew in a deep breath. "As you say, Rob, there is nothing either of us can do. Except leave her alone."

"Exactly."

The door closed on Charles, and Lord Menteith sat down behind his desk, his eyes on the pile of papers waiting for his attention. He picked up a memo and sat regarding it intently, but his mind was still on his recent conversation with his brother. Charles had surprised him. Evidently he did not regard with distaste the prospect of a relationship between his well-loved sister and Adam Todd, Viscount Stanford.

Gacé, usually so observant, was too preoccupied with
his own affairs to notice the change in his wife. He had
written several letter to friends and relations in Baden
and Frankfurt and was satisfied that Baden was indeed
the best place for him to be in the near future. No matter what happened in Europe, Gacé had decided that it
would be best to sever his ties to England.

He had not yet given up on Napoleon and planned to
devote a few more months to the Horse Guards and
Stanford in the hope of getting some information about
the Spanish campaign. If he was able to pass valuable
plans along to Paris and Napoleon won decisively in
Spain, the emperor's large, veteran army would be freed
for service in Germany. The English would of course realize that Napoleon had been given advance warning of
Wellington's plans, but Gacé would be safely in Baden
by then.

If Napoleon won, Gacé would have everything he
wanted. But if Napoleon lost . . . The possibility of such
a catastrophe was seeming less and less remote to the
concerned Gacé, and he devoted a great deal of his time
to the securing of his own position should such an event
actually happen.

His greatest fear was exposure. Not many French officials knew who their English source was, but those who
did know would scarcely keep quiet about it once they
were defeated. As soon as the allies marched into Paris
and started talking to the surviving government, his
name was certain to come up. It would definitely come
up if Louis sent him, as he most probably would want
to, to Paris as one of his own representatives.

The problems facing Gacé might have seemed
awesome, but with the ruthless egotism that lay under
his cultured exterior, he set himself to resolve them. The
only thing that mattered to Gacé was the name and the
honor of the name of de Vaudobin.

The solution, as he thought about it, was really quite

simple. It was true that Gacé's name was known to Napoleon and to a few other officials in Paris, but no one, with the exception of François Bellay, his courier, had ever seen him. He would deny everything and say someone else had been passing the information and using his name. To ensure the success of this plan required only two things: the death of Bellay and a scapegoat to take the blame as the real traitor.

The first problem, Bellay's death, would be easy enough to accomplish. As for the second, Gacé did not foresee too many difficulties there either. He cast about in his mind for a likely candidate at the Horse Guards. He needed someone high enough up to have access to information and, preferably, someone who had financial problems that the selling of information to the French might alleviate. Gacé finally settled on the Earl of Denham, a peer whose gambling debts were notorious. With polished ease Gacé began to insinuate himself into the good graces of Denham, a man to whom he had hitherto paid scant attention. It was also necessary for him to prepare the king for any future accusations that might be made against his most trusted friend and advisor.

With this in mind, Gacé began spending more time than usual at Hartwell. With great discretion he hinted to the king that all was not well at the Horse Guards; information, he feared, was leaking to Bonaparte. Sorrowfully he confided his own fear of being suspected if the English did in truth start to search for a traitor. He had never been fully accepted by *les Anglais*. Everyone knew they distrusted all Frenchmen. . . .

The king was indignant. And reassuring. He, at least, would never distrust his dear friend Monseigneur de Gacé.

At the end of March, Gacé went to Hartwell for a private dinner with his majesty. He informed Nanda that he would stay the night and return the next day. It was the opportunity Stanford had been waiting for.

Nanda had not been alarmed by Gacé's announce-
ment. She was engaged for dinner and the theater that
evening. The organizer of the party was her sister-in-law
Helen, Lady Menteith, who had arrived from Scotland
at the beginning of March. Helen, doubtless warned by
Menteith, had not invited Lord Stanford, and Nanda felt
secure in the knowledge that she would be returned
home in her brother's carriage and could then go straight
to bed. She would not see Stanford at all.

The earlier part of the evening went according to
Nanda's plan. At Menteith House she found, beside her
brother and sister-in-law, Sir George and Lady Murray,
Major and Mrs. Munro, and, to escort her, Sir Alistair
Hepburn. They were all old friends, cosmopolitan Scots
who still retained their ties to home, and Nanda relaxed
and enjoyed herself as she had not done in weeks.
Kemble was playing at Covent Garden, and the play was
excellent. The Menteiths and Sir Alistair saw her home,
and the night footman let her into the house at about one
in the morning. There was no sign of Stanford, and,
thankfully, Nanda went upstairs. She allowed her maid
to undress her in silence and got into bed, relaxed and
drowsy as she had not been for a long time. She was just
slipping off to sleep when her bedroom door opened.
Startled, she sat up only to see Stanford, a candle in his
hand, closing the door behind him. He set the candle
down on the mahogany table next to the bed and looked
into her startled eyes. "What are you doing here?" she
demanded, anger, surprise, and fear sounding alterna-
tively in her voice.

Chapter 14

Still, I swear I love you.
—*Cymbeline*, II, iii, 95

Stanford's face was composed as he stood beside her bed looking steadily into her face. His arms were at his sides, the hands relaxed and open. He made no attempt to touch her. "I came for two reasons," he said quietly. "The first was to ask you a question."

The candle threw its light over the bed, showing her straight back, long, glossy hair, and great dark eyes. "A question?" she repeated. "What question is so urgent that you must needs break into my bedroom to ask it?"

There was two feet between him and the bed, and, as he spoke in the same quiet voice, he refrained from coming any closer. "If you were sure of getting custody of Marc and Ginny, would you divorce Gacé and marry me?" he said.

There was a stunned silence as she regarded him speechlessly. "There is no possibility of that ever happening," she answered finally.

"But if there were?"

There was no urgency in his voice. He might have been discussing the weather, she thought wildly. Then she met his eyes, and the utter intensity of his gaze shook her profoundly. It was totally at variance with the level calmness of his voice. That voice, under such strict control, said again, "If Gacé gave up the children, would you divorce him and marry me?"

Divorce, as they both knew, was not unheard of in

their world, but it was a stigma. A divorced woman would be barred from the very highest level of society, the level Nanda now inhabited—indeed, helped to rule. She took an uneven breath. "Yes," she said. "I would divorce him and marry you."

He felt himself start to breathe again, and Nanda saw the color return to his face. His eyes made a mockery of his relaxed, easy posture. The last anger drained from her, and she looked at him with questioning eyes. He was still in evening dress, but he had removed his coat and neckcloth. His hair and skin looked dark against the white of his open-necked shirt. "Why do you ask me this?" she asked softly.

He made no answer, but smiled at her with a curious gravity. She thought suddenly that he had the most beautiful mouth she had ever seen. "There is no chance, Adam," she repeated breathlessly.

"I don't know."

She leaned a little forward, a slight frown between the delicate wings of her brows. "Something is wrong, isn't it?" she said sharply. "With Matthieu, I mean."

He looked genuinely surprised. "Why do you say that?"

"I don't know. It's just something I've felt. He's disturbed about something."

There was a long pause. "Is he?" Stanford looked at her thoughtfully.

"Yes, he is." She compressed her lips. "You're not going to tell me anything, are you?"

For the first time he moved closer to the bed. "No," he said gently. "In this, Nanda, you will have to trust me."

The column of his neck looked very bronzed and strong where it rose above his opened shirt. "You said you came for two reasons," she said breathlessly.

"Yes. The first was to ask you a question." He took

another step forward so he stood now directly beside the bed. "The second was to make love to you."

The light from the candle struck a gleam of deep blue from under his lashes. Her throat ached and her heart began to thud. "No," she whispered.

"You don't understand, my darling," he said. "You have no choice." And, turning her face up with gentle fingers, he bent his head and began to kiss her, long and slowly.

At his touch she went totally still, trying to deny the intense response that flooded through her. "You have no choice," he had said, but the part of her that still could think knew that if she resisted him he would let her go. She put up a hand to push him away and felt his lips move from her mouth to the hollow of her throat. He was pressing her backward. With a long, shuddering sigh she allowed him to lay her down, and the hand she had raised to push him away buried itself, caressingly, in his crisp black hair.

Gacé was a skilled lover, but she had not known love could be like this. His hands and his mouth caressed and wooed her until she felt like a piece of delicate crystal reverberating with the piercing high notes of a finely played flute. She held him to her and felt him move: higher and higher until she could bear it no longer and dug her nails into the strength of his back until the shattering waves of fulfillment broke over her and she cried out.

Afterward she lay beside him, her hair spread on the pillow, a dark frame for the glowing beauty of her face. He raised himself on an elbow and watched her, his own face relaxed and youthful, his eyes brilliant under the open black lashes. She raised a hand to touch his cheek. "That wasn't fair," she said softly.

"Why?" His voice was deeper than usual.

"Because I was ready to give you up."

He bent his head so that his lips touched the smooth, warm curve of her throat. "And now?" he murmured.

Her smile was blinding. "What do you think?"

"What I have always thought: there is no escape. Not from this."

Her eyes were dark pools in the fine-boned perfection of her face. "No," she agreed softly. "Not from this." Her voice caught slightly. "I didn't know."

His firm, sensitive mouth curved in a smile so intimate it sent shivers through her. "I had a dream," he said, "but it pales beside the reality."

"Adam." Her voice trembled with suppressed emotion. "I love you so. What are we going to do?"

"I can't tell you, Nanda, but believe me, everything will be all right. Trust me, my love."

Her great eyes searched his face for a clue. He met her gaze fully, his own eyes open and clear. "Don't you know by now that I love you?" he said quietly. "I would cut out my heart before I hurt you."

She laughed shakenly. "I don't care if you hurt me. Just so long as you love me."

As she spoke his eyes narrowed and he reached out to slide his hands into the shining silk of her hair. "Forever," he said, and covered her mouth with his.

"Trust me," Stanford had said, and Nanda made up her mind to do just that. She knew that if ever she gave way to the fears and doubts that lodged deep within her soul they would drown her joy. And she was joyful. It astonished her that she, who had been a slave to conscience all her life, could be so happy in an illicit love affair. There was a singing inside of her that translated into a luminous glow that shone in her eyes and even from the delicate tones of her skin. Whenever she saw Stanford or even heard his voice, her heart lurched and she felt dizzy with happiness.

She wanted to be with him. She wanted to touch him. She wanted him to touch her. Face it, she thought to herself one blustery afternoon as she sat in the green saloon, a piece of embroidery held uselessly in her hands, you want him to make love to you.

It had been over a week since the night Stanford had come to her room, and no other opportunities had come their way. Gacé was home again, which made Berkeley Square much too dangerous for a lovers' rendezvous. Nanda, to her own horror, found herself trying to think of other places where they might safely meet.

I never thought I could behave like this, she thought as she stared distractedly at her neglected embroidery. They had been at the same ball last evening, and she remembered vividly how the sight of him across the room had affected her. He had been talking to Lord Henry Staples and had suddenly thrown back his head, laughter lighting the usual reserved stillness of his face. A rowel of pain had knifed through her, a need so intense it took her breath and hurt her throat.

She felt that pain again, sitting alone by the fire, and did not hear the sound of steps in the hall until the door opened and Virginie looked in. "There you are, Mama!" she said and came in and seated herself next to Nanda on the sofa. "We had such a good time."

With an effort Nanda focused her attention on her stepdaughter. Ginny had spent the afternoon with Lady Menteith and her daughter Margaret, who was almost the same age as Ginny. She listened to the little girl's excited chatter with half an ear, until Ginny said the words "dueling exhibition."

"What was that, darling?" She frowned.

"We saw a dueling exhibition. It was great fun, Mama. Meggie and I both decided it would be excessively romantic to have a duel fought over us. With swords, of course. Just like Sir Lancelot and the Lady Guinevere."

Nanda smiled and nodded and exclaimed; all the while

her heart felt frozen with fear. "I hope you remembered to thank Aunt Helen for taking you," she said finally.

Ginny looked slightly affronted. "Of course I did, Mama."

"Good girl," Nanda said absently. "Run along now, Miss Braxton is waiting for you."

After Ginny had left, Nanda sat on for another half an hour until the servants came to light the lamps. The song within her was silent, effectively quenched by the idea Ginny's words had put in her mind. "Everything will be all right," Stanford had promised.

"Dear God," Nanda whispered, her eyes black with fear. "He can't mean to call Matthieu out?"

Chapter 15

His meanest garment,
That ever hath but clipped his body, is dearer
In my respect than all the hairs above thee,
Were they all made such men.
—*Cymbeline*, II, iii, 138-41

Stanford spent the week following his night with Nanda in preparing his case against her husband. When he had organized his evidence in as coldly purposeful a fashion as was possible under the circumstances, he went to see the military secretary, who also happened to be Robert Doune, Lord Menteith, Nanda's brother.

They met at Menteith's town house in Hanover Square, behind the firmly closed door of his lordship's library. There, amid the background of leatherbound books and big, comfortable armchairs, Stanford felt safer opening such an explosive topic than he would at the Horse Guards.

Menteith sat before a pleasantly crackling fire, opposite the chair Stanford had been given. His eyes took in the quiet, relaxed figure of Adam Todd, his empty hands and reserved face. "I apprehend you have news for me, Stanford," he said courteously.

Stanford looked gravely back. He liked Lord Menteith. During his months at the Horse Guards he had come to respect his integrity, his patience, and his ability. It was vitally important to convince him of the truth about Gacé. "I have found your traitor," Stanford began.

"I see." Lord Menteith's pleasant face looked distinctly apprehensive. "Who?"

Stanford's voice was colorless. "The Duc de Gacé, I regret to inform you."

"What!" Menteith thrust himself upright, his hands on the arms of his big chair. Angrily he stared at Adam Todd. "You must be mistaken!"

"Please sit down, my lord," Stanford responded quietly. "I am afraid it is true. I realize you may have cause to doubt my motives about Gacé, but I hope the evidence I am about to present will be convincing."

Slowly Menteith sank back into his chair, his eyes never leaving Stanford's face. He chose to ignore, for the moment, the first part of Stanford's speech and replied only to his last statement, "It had better be, Stanford. I am not inclined to take such an accusation against my brother-in-law lightly." There was a harsh line between Menteith's brows and a challenge in his brown eyes.

"I realize that, my lord," Stanford answered, his hands lying quietly on the arms of his chair. "It is not an accusation I make lightly, I assure you."

For a moment Menteith continued to stare at him, then he made a movement with his hand. "All right," he said tightly, apparently satisfied with what he saw. "Tell me."

Stanford turned his gaze into the flames of the fire blazing so briskly in the beautiful Adam fireplace and began. His voice was deliberate, calm, and uninflected. "You thought it was strange, did you not, when Gacé invited me to be a guest in his home? I did also." Stanford's eyes left the fire and went to Menteith's face. "Why did he do that, my lord?" he asked softly.

"A charitable impulse," Menteith answered, his face wooden.

A spark of genuine amusement gleamed in the blue eyes of Adam Todd. "I very much doubt that Matthieu de Vaudobin ever in his life suffered from anything so awkward as a charitable impulse." His voice was dry.

Menteith's eyes fell. "Why, then, did he invite you, Stanford?"

"To give himself ample opportunity to pick my brain about the spring campaign. Which he did, assiduously."

"Gacé's interest in the spring campaign is not evidence, Stanford." Menteith's voice was harsh. "There are many possible reasons for his curiosity."

"Perhaps. But it was enough to raise my suspicions." The level, easy tone of Stanford's voice never varied. He might have been discussing a dinner menu. "I was also intrigued by the voluminous amount of Gacé's mail," he continued. "It came from all over Europe. It proved to be very interesting reading."

"You read his mail?" Genuine horror sounded in Menteith's voice.

For the first time a hint of impatience crossed Stanford's face. "One can hardly engage in intelligence work and observe the rules of etiquette at the same time, my lord. If you had spent less time at the Horse Guards observing the social amenities and more time on security you would not have had information handed to the French with such alarming regularity. And a number of men I knew who are now dead would be alive and well."

Menteith flushed and looked away from the sudden bitter anger that had flared in Stanford's eyes. "What did you find in his mail?" he asked, ignoring Stanford's last statement, since there was obviously no reply he could make.

"His grace's mail makes our own diplomatic channels look paltry. Furthermore, he has had access to information that would have been useful to us, and he did not communicate it."

There was a pause. "And then?" Menteith grated.

Stanford removed his gaze from Menteith's face and

stared back at the fire. "I had him followed. Then I fed him some information that would have been of interest to Paris." Stanford paused a moment, then went on smoothly. "He met with a Frenchman named Bellay in a bookstore in Piccadilly. The information was passed in a book Gacé had been holding. This happened three times. The last time I had Bellay followed. He traveled immediately to Folkestone, where he met with the captain of a fishing vessel. The boat sailed on the next tide. Bellay returned to London, where he has lodgings near the river."

Menteith said nothing. The silence stretched on. If he had not been convinced, Stanford thought, his case would be desperate indeed. The only hope of saving Nanda from the consequences of Gacé's treason lay in convincing her brother. He needed Menteith's aid in accomplishing his plan. The lines around his mouth were grim as he said, "I said I had evidence, but it is not enough to convict. To stop Gacé, I will need your help."

A log cracked and fell on the fire. Finally Menteith cleared his throat and spoke. "No," he said.

There was nothing in Stanford's face to betray the bitterness of his failure, but the knuckles on his quiet hands showed suddenly white. "Why not?" he asked.

"Because of Nanda, of course," her brother said violently. "The scandal would be intolerable. For her, for the children most of all. Their father hanged as a traitor! They would never recover from it."

The wild relief Stanford felt showed only in the quickly checked gesture of his hand. When he finally spoke his voice was carefully controlled. "Why do you think I asked to see you alone? And here, at your home?"

Menteith turned to stare at him. "Do you have an idea, Stanford?"

"Yes."

Menteith thrust his hand through his hair. "We cannot try Gacé for treason," he said stubbornly.

"I agree."

Menteith looked at the composed face of Stanford, his own bewildered. "Why did he do it? He has a good position. He doesn't need money."

Stanford laughed unpleasantly. "Your brother Charles could tell you, Menteith. He said to me once that to Gacé the restoration of his own lands and prestige far outweigh the restoration of the monarchy." Stanford frowned thoughtfully. "I think Gacé got tired of waiting. Since Louis was unable to give him back his own, he decided to try Napoleon. He doesn't care who wins the war; he only cares that Matthieu de Vaudobin should end up with the Chateau de Gacé. His egotism is colossal, you know."

"I know." Menteith suddenly looked much older. "I never should have allowed Nanda to marry him. It is the biggest cross of my life that I did so."

"She would not agree with you," Stanford said flatly.

For a long moment Menteith stared into the dark face of the young man opposite him. For once Stanford made no effort to guard his eyes. 'So Charles was right," Menteith said finally. "You do love her."

"I had not realized I was quite so obvious," Stanford said astringently.

"Charles has always had a sixth sense about Nanda," Menteith said. "They have always been close to each other, and Charles has become even more protective since her marriage."

"I see."

Menteith frowned. "No, you don't see. Charles only wants Nanda's happiness. If you can make her happy, Stanford, you will have his blessing. And mine." The earl leaned forward slightly. "But for everyone's sake," he said meaningfully, "it must be marriage."

"It will be."

"How?"

Stanford told him.

When he had finished there was a little silence. "Do you think Matthieu will agree to what you propose?"

Stanford's eyes narrowed. "Really, Menteith, he will have no choice."

Menteith looked at the merciless face of the young man seated so calmly in his library chair. "No," he said slowly, "I don't suppose he will."

The evening after her conversation with Ginny, Nanda and Gacé attended a ball given by Lord and Lady Crosby, Stanford's aunt and uncle. The Crosbys were not of the political coterie Gacé belonged to, being devoted to the principles of the late Charles James Fox, but they had invited Gacé because of Stanford, and, because of Stanford, the duc had accepted.

Lady Crosby had filled her rooms with all the great landowning Whig aristocracy, and even Gacé's snobbery was soothed by the amount of blue blood present. He stayed close to Nanda during the first hour of the evening, looking stiff and reserved, but when Lord Grenville, who was even stiffer than Gacé, came to draw him aside, he went willingly.

Lady Crosby came across the room during a break in the sets to speak to Nanda. "Anthony, my dear, would you be good enough to bring me a glass of champagne?" she said to Lord Charlton, ruthlessly annexing his seat next to Nanda. "Now, my dear," Lady Crosby said when a reluctant Lord Charlton had gone, "I must thank you for taking such excellent care of Adam. From what my brother wrote to me I had expected to find him a sad case indeed." Her bright-gray eyes looked shrewdly at Nanda.

"You must thank Lord Stanford's excellent constitution, Lady Crosby," Nanda said, "not me."

"He was always strong as a horse, though you wouldn't think it to look at him," Lady Crosby agreed. "And he is working with your husband at the Horse Guards?"

Nanda's back was very straight. "I believe Lord Stanford is working with my brother, Lady Crosby, though my husband is attached to the Horse Guards as well."

"My, your family is certainly involved in the war effort," Lady Crosby was beginning, her voice slightly malicious, when a deeper voice cut across hers. "I have come to escort her grace to the supper room, Aunt Frances," Stanford said firmly. "I have procured champagne for all your dowagers and been polite to at least three unattractive girls. I am now going to please myself and have supper with the duchesse."

Lady Crosby's eyebrows were slightly raised. "It may please you to have supper with the duchesse, Adam, but does it please her to have supper with you?" She turned to Nanda and said lightly, "You needn't go with him, my dear, unless you want to."

The dusky glow in Nanda's cheeks was somewhat heightened, but she answered composedly enough, "I should be delighted to have supper with Lord Stanford." She rose and put her hand on his arm, looking fleetingly up at him from under her long lashes. He was watching her, and the meeting of their eyes was like a stolen caress.

Lady Crosby watched them cross the room together, a slight frown between her brows. That glance had told her all she wanted to know.

It is serious with him this time, she thought worriedly. Lady Crosby had known her nephew since his childhood, and that knowledge was what was causing her such severe concern at the moment. Adam was not the kind to concern himself with public opinion; he did only what *he* thought he should do. If he loved Nanda de Vaudobin, his aunt thought distractedly, God alone knew what he would be prepared to do about it. Adam was not the sort of man who would be willing to share the woman he loved with another man, even if that man happened to be her husband. Nor was he the sort of man to give up. Lady Crosby's enjoyment in her own ball was quite effectively destroyed by that one nakedly revealing glance she had seen pass between her nephew and the Duchesse de Gacé.

Stanford had made a detour on his way to the supper room, and he steered Nanda into a small anteroom and closed the door firmly behind them. In a moment she was in his arms, his mouth hard and hungry on hers. She closed her eyes and leaned against him, heedless of how he was crushing her gown.

It was he who made the move to separate them. "God, Nanda," his voice was harsh. "I must see you alone."

"How?" Her lips barely moved.

"I have the key to a cottage in Hampstead." He gave her the address. "Will you come?"

"Yes."

"Tomorrow?"

Her eyes were huge and black, almost engulfing the rest of her face. "Yes," she breathed again.

"Two o'clock. Take a hackney."

"All right."

There was the sound of voices outside the room, then there was silence. "We'd better go," said Stanford.

She nodded and took a step toward the door. "Adam!" Her voice was suddenly strong and urgent. "You aren't planning to call Matthieu out, are you?"

His eyes widened in surprise. "Why should you think that?"

She gestured helplessly. "You said that everything would come out all right for us, and I was afraid . . ."

"You were afraid I'd kill Gacé in a duel?" There was a touch of incredulity in his voice.

"There are two people who may be killed in a duel," she reminded him breathlessly, and this time the fear in her eyes was unmistakable.

He saw it. "I have no intention of fighting a duel with Gacé," he said reasonably. "In the first place, I can hardly challenge him. One can't call a man out because one happens to love his wife. He, of course, could always challenge me, but I don't think he would want that kind of scandal."

She was frowning. "No. He wouldn't."

"So you may rest easy, my love. No one knows better than I that Gacé's death would solve all our problems. Believe me, I have thought of it." His mouth was like iron. "But, under the circumstances, I don't feel I am the one who can do it." He opened the door for her to precede him into the hall. "Unfortunately," he added to himself.

Chapter 16

Then, true Pisanio—
Who long'st, like me, to see thy lord; who long'st—
Oh, let me bate—but not like me—yet long'st,
But in a fainter kind—oh, not like me,
For mine's beyond beyond . . .

—*Cymbeline*, III, ii, 54-58

The April sun was clear and warm, shining brightly on the streets of London, when Amanda de Vaudobin, Duchesse de Gacé, got into a hackney carriage for the first time in her life. She scarcely noticed her changing surroundings as the cab left the city environs and entered the village of Hampstead. Finally it stopped before a low, whitewashed cottage, surrounded by a garden filled with daffodils.

Nanda gave the man two guineas. "If you will come back for me in two hours, there will be two more guineas for you," she told him.

The driver looked at the beautiful woman whose elegant green pelisse and broad-brimmed hat clearly proclaimed Quality. She was up to no good, he surmised, but that was no affair of his. Two guineas was two guineas. "Aye, I'll be back," he said, and tipped his hat.

She waited until he was out of sight, then turned, opened the white picket fence and walked toward the cottage. A part of her seemed to stand aside and watch, unbelievingly, as she advanced steadily down the path toward her lover. "I must be mad!" that small, sane part of her cried in protest; but she walked on, heedless of its warning.

The door opened and he was waiting there, and the look on his face as he saw her caught at her throat. She crossed the threshold into the low-ceilinged, immaculate room and was in his arms.

They lay in a wide bed, under the roof, with the sun streaming in the window dappling their skin. Nanda's head was on Stanford's shoulder, her long hair falling across his chest.

"However did you find this lovely cottage?" she asked, her voice rich with contentment.

His fingers slowly caressed the smooth, bare skin of her arm. "I rented it."

There was a hint of amusement in her voice. "Ever efficient."

He touched her hair with his lips. "I know."

She heaved a sigh of satisfaction. "This is dreadfully immoral," she offered.

"Mmn?" Clearly his mind was elsewhere. "Nanda?"

There was a note of strain in his voice, and, surprised, she turned her head to look at him. "What is it, Adam?"

There was a pinched look about Stanford's nostrils as he looked at the beautiful, glowing face bent above him. "I swore I wouldn't ask you this," he said, his voice hard and rough. "I have no right."

"Ask me what, my love?"

"Has Gacé made love to you since . . ." His voice trailed off as the light died from her eyes. She lay back on the pillow and looked at the ceiling.

He cursed. She had never heard anyone swear like that before. Then he raised himself to look down at her. "I'm sorry, my darling. I'm a damned fool to have asked you that."

"No, you were not a damned fool. And no, Matthieu has not touched me."

The relief he felt flooding him left him momentarily

without words. After a few moments' silence, he spoke gently. "Then why do you look like that?"

"I said that this is immoral, Adam, but it isn't. It is my marriage to Matthieu that is immoral. How can I remain his wife when I feel as I do about you?" She returned his gaze gravely. "And Matthieu is not stupid. If I keep denying him he will suspect something." There was a pause, then she added with difficulty, "He came to my room two nights ago. I sent him away, but he will come back."

His face was drawn and bleak in the harsh sunlight. "A month," he said. "In one month's time it should all be finished and you and I can be married."

"And you are not going to kill Matthieu?" Her voice was sharp with alarm.

"No. I am not going to kill Matthieu." He reached out a hand to touch her cheek. "I think it better not to tell you, Nanda. You have enough to hide from Gacé as it is."

"Yes, perhaps it is better if I do not," she agreed slowly, her great eyes searching his face. She turned her head so that her lips touched his hand. "I must go," she whispered.

He kissed her throat. "Not yet," he muttered.

Her hands buried themselves in his thick, black hair. "No. Not yet."

As the days and weeks passed, Nanda's life became but a waiting from hour to hour, between the hours when she saw Stanford at the cottage and the empty time in between. With grim resolution she pushed aside all her other considerations and responsibilities. There would be time enough in a month to face the thought of all else in her life save this man she loved. In her anxious, passionate heart, she doubted that any real future stretched before them. In a month she would know. For now she could not bear to lose an hour of the time that was left them together.

They were discreet. They rarely attended the same social function, and when they did they never arrived together. Indeed, for the first time in their five years of marriage, Gacé had become his wife's steady escort. Nanda feared he was suspicious about her relationship with Stanford. If he did discover her affair, she was not sure how he would take it. She had a suspicion that, for all his aristocratic cynicism, he would not like it. It was not that he cared about her himself; it was more his sense of proprietorship that would be outraged.

Gacé was not the only one to suspect, if suspect he did. Their very avoidance of each other gave them away. And when they did meet their polite, cool voices and resolutely impersonal eyes were belied by the almost tangible current that seemed to crackle between them.

Charles Doune, for one, was not fooled. He was standing at a reception at Lady Edgecomb's one evening talking to Miss Marrenby when Stanford came in. Charles noticed how his eyes swept quickly around the room, almost instantly locating Nanda. She turned, as if she had felt his glance, and their eyes met briefly. Then Stanford turned away and went to speak to Colonel Torrens.

Elizabeth Marrenby had observed exactly the same thing as Charles, and she looked now at his handsome face, which was slightly puckered with a frown. "Your sister is so beautiful, Mr. Doune," she said in her soft voice. "There is a kind of light shining out of her." She hesitated, then went on, "It is the light of goodness, I have always thought."

Charles' fine dark eyes looked thoughtfully at the lovely face of Miss Marrenby. "It surprises me to hear you say that," he said, questioningly. Elizabeth Marrenby's partiality for Stanford had not escaped Charles either.

A slight flush rose in her porcelain cheeks. "When I

first came to London, last year, I was very unhappy. Mama knew so few people, you see, and I . . ." She broke off, in some confusion.

"I understand perfectly," Charles said dryly. He had forgotten Nanda's role in bringing this girl to the attention of the ton. He was slightly surprised that Elizabeth, now an accredited toast, still remembered Nanda's kindness with so much gratitude. For the first time he looked at her with genuine interest, seeing not an heiress or an accredited beauty, but a nice girl who was aware of his distress and had tried to help. He began to see why Nanda had bothered with her. He smiled at her more warmly than he had yet done. "Would you care to drive in the park with me tomorrow afternoon, Miss Marrenby?" he asked, as two other young gentlemen bore down on them.

She gave him her sweet smile. "I should love to, Mr. Doune."

While Charles, in his worry, turned more and more to the gentle and soothing company of Elizabeth Marrenby, Lady Crosby took more definite action. She had no objection to her nephew's conducting a discreet affair with the Duchesse de Gacé, but her intuition, always keen when it came to matters of the heart, had been alerted by that look she had seen Nanda and Stanford exchange at her ball. The passion contained in that look was the stuff that ripped apart the very fabric of social life. Lady Crosby had been born a Todd and she was not going to stand by while her brother's heir, the future head of the family, did something that might bring about his own social ostracism.

She had called on Nanda one morning, and that interview had done little to ameliorate her worry. Nanda was calm and polite, but there was a look of radiance about her that made Lady Crosby extremely nervous. A woman who looked like that would be capable of anything. Including eloping with Viscount Stanford, Lord Wellington's protégé and heir to the Earl of Dunstanburgh.

In Lady Crosby's memory the only person who had ever had any influence over Adam was his father. Reluctantly, Lady Crosby decided to write to her brother.

Chapter 17

. . . if there be
Yet left in heaven as small a drop of pity
As a wren's eye, feared gods, a part of it!
—*Cymbeline*, IV, ii, 303-05

Stanford was unaware of the stir his love affair was causing in the breasts of his apprehensive family as he met with Menteith in the library of the earl's house in Hanover Square to plan the downfall of the Duc de Gacé. The two men sat on either side of Menteith's beautifully polished desk. Stanford spoke first, in a calm unhurried tone.

"I think I will let him steal a memorandum, Menteith. As I said to you earlier, we need a solid piece of evidence, and a stolen memorandum containing secret information is certainly that."

Menteith stared at the sculptured face of the younger man. The eyes that returned his look were remote and calculating. "Dash it, Stanford," Menteith protested. "You aren't proposing to give him real information?"

Stanford's answer was reasonable. "We have no choice. We can hardly prosecute him for passing false information. And unless we give him something valuable, Gacé is not likely to risk sending it at all. I rather think our friend the duc is having uncomfortable doubts about Boney's future. I shouldn't be at all surprised to discover he was looking for a way to change sides again."

Lord Menteith ran his hand through his hair. "What do you have in mind?" he asked uneasily.

Stanford picked up a jeweled paperknife from the

desk top and began to turn it over and over in his fingers. With his eyes on his hands he said slowly, "I will draw up a memorandum pertaining to the new supply route and have it ready to put on my desk. The next time Gacé comes into my office I shall leave it there and make an excuse to go out for just a few minutes. When I come back I rather doubt the memorandum will still be where I left it."

"How will you prove he took it?"

Stanford looked up, a faint, sardonic smile on his lips. "I will keep an eye on the door of my office."

"I see." Menteith cleared his throat. "You will be able to swear that the memorandum was there when you left the room and gone when you returned. And the only person in the room will have been Gacé."

"Precisely."

Menteith's kind brown eyes looked worriedly at Stanford. "And then?"

"Then." Stanford put the paperknife down and loosely laced his hands together. His voice was grave. "Then, we keep my lord duc under constant surveillance. I am quite sure he will pass the memorandum on to Bellay. It is imperative that Bellay be stopped and the memorandum recovered. Do you have men picked out to do that?"

Menteith frowned. "Yes, I know who I want."

"Good. They must stop Bellay and bring him to you. You promise him a reasonable prison term instead of the gallows if he will sign a paper swearing that Gacé has been passing him secret information for the last eight months." Stanford unclasped his hands and reached into his pocket. "Then we will confront Gacé with the evidence. *And* these documents I had drawn up by my solicitor."

Menteith took the documents and read them. The first was a confession of espionage. The second was a statement in which Gacé agreed to Nanda's divorcing him and in which he relinquished to her the permanent guardianship of his children, Virginie and Marc.

Menteith looked up from the legal papers he held in his hands. "Supposing he signs these, we still can't let him go. He will have read the memorandum. What do we do with him then?"

I know what I should like to do with him, Stanford thought grimly. But, looking at the kind, worried face of the Earl of Menteith, he knew he could not suggest what he had in mind. The whole Doune family, he thought wryly, appeared to be burdened by extremely strict consciences.

He leaned back a little in his chair. "We cannot let him go right away, certainly. I suggest we place him under our personal detention, preferably somewhere in Scotland. Once the opening maneuvers are over this spring, we will release him and help him leave the country. We will give it out that he has already left when he is, in fact, in Scotland. There will be some speculation, but nothing so damaging as a trial and a hanging. It is, I believe, the neatest solution, under the circumstances." Stanford's eyes were as cold as winter. "I think Gacé will behave himself. We will be holding his signed confession."

Lord Menteith had been painstakingly following Stanford's words, a slight frown on his face. When Stanford concluded the earl gave a slight nod. "It sounds all right. I can send him to my castle in Fife. He should be safe enough there. But, for God's sake, Stanford, we must be sure to recover that memorandum!"

"We will," said Stanford coolly. "Gacé has no suspicions he has been detected. And he thinks I'm a fool. That is his weak point. He is correct about his own cleverness, but he underestimates everyone else. That was the mistake he made with Nanda."

There was a pause, then Menteith said heavily, "When?"

"As soon as possible. Gacé has not been at the Horse Guards much lately. He spends most of his time at Hartwell, trying to turn the king up sweet, I suppose. I'll prepare the memorandum and have it ready the next time he pays me a visit."

"Very well," Lord Menteith said resignedly. "You will let me know as soon as Gacé makes his move?"

"I will let you know," Stanford said stonily.

The plan was put into effect exactly four days after Stanford had met with Menteith. Stanford was sitting before his neatly piled desk when the door opened and the duc came in. "Gacé," said Stanford, a note of surprise in his voice. "We haven't seen you around here for quite some time."

"No, I have been in attendance upon his majesty a great deal lately. You appear to be as busy as ever, dear boy." Gacé gestured gracefully toward the loaded desk.

"As you see," Stanford said ruefully. "In fact I have another report to pick up from Menteith. He is going out shortly and I don't want to miss him. Do you mind waiting for just a moment?"

Something flickered in Gacé's eyes. "Not at all," he said smoothly.

Stanford went out, but he didn't go to Menteith's office. He stayed where he could keep an eye on his door. He waited five minutes. No one went in or went out. Then he extracted a piece of paper from his breast pocket and returned to his own office.

Gacé was standing at the window, looking out at rain-swept Whitehall. He turned as Stanford came in. "I have never been able to adjust to your English weather," he said lightly. "So much rain."

"This is nothing," said Stanford. "You should have seen the rain at Burgos."

"Ah, yes," Gacé responded with ready sympathy.

"England must seem snug indeed, after that." He walked to the middle of the room. "Well, I won't intrude on your time any longer, my dear boy. You are, as I mentioned, well occupied. My wife and I are dining at the Liverpools' this evening. Shall we see you there?"

"No, Gacé. I have not yet breached the prime minister's circle."

"The Crosbys *are* very outspoken," Gacé said softly. "Well, I will leave you to your work, Stanford. Adieu."

Stanford waited three minutes before he looked at his desk. It looked untouched. But the memorandum was gone. He went to tell Menteith.

The next afternoon the Earl of Dunstanburgh reached London and went directly to the Grosvenor Square residence of his sister. Happily, she was in.

"Now what is this all about, Frances?" he grumbled as he stumped around her smart drawing room, stretching his travel-cramped legs.

"Do sit down, Richard," Lady Crosby responded. "You make me nervous when you circle around like that."

He came to stand before the fire and propped his shoulders against the Wedgwood mantel. "I don't want to sit down," he said. "I've been sitting for days in that damn chaise. Now, tell me, Frances," he repeated patiently, "what this is all about."

"It's about Adam," she said with some asperity. "I wrote you about it, Richard. He has been staying at the Duc de Gacé's house in Berkeley Square and while there has fallen in love with the duchesse."

"Women have been chasing Adam since he was sixteen," said the earl dispassionately, "and Adam never ran very fast. You know that."

"Yes, but this is different." Her eyes narrowed. "This is *dangerous*, Richard. There is a recklessness about this that disturbs me greatly."

"You think he's serious, then?"

"I think he is deadly serious."

"What about the woman?"

"I have never known Nanda de Vaudobin personally, but of course I have seen and heard of her for years. She is quite probably the most beautiful woman I have ever seen. And she is virtuous. Until now, there has never been any gossip about the Duchesse de Gacé."

There was a frown between the earl's iron-gray brows. "Is there gossip, now?"

"There is beginning to be some." Lady Crosby leaned forward in her rosewood chair. "It is not the gossip that worries me, Richard. If they are having an affair, and I am sure they are, they are being discreet. But this has the look of something more than an affair. To be frank, I'm afraid they will elope together."

The earl swore softly. "Damme, Frances, if he does that the boy's finished. He has a brilliant future—dash it, I wouldn't be surprised if he ended up prime minister one day!"

"Well, he won't if he elopes with the Duc de Gacé's wife," his sister said drily.

The earl paced to the window, then back again. "I can talk to him, Frances, but I doubt if he'll listen."

"Nonsense, Richard," she said briskly, "dear Adam has always been very fond of you."

The earl looked suddenly older. "I know he is fond of me, Frances, and perhaps I didn't phrase my thought correctly. He will listen to me; I do not ever remember Adam refusing to do that. And if he feels it is possible to go along with my request, he will. But if his mind is made up, nothing I can say will change him. He is not a boy any longer." The earl came and sat down on a curve-legged sofa. "I don't know anything about Gacé," he said heavily. "Is his wife French, too?"

"No. She is a Doune. Menteith's her elder brother."

"A Doune. It is hard to imagine one of that family doing anything so rash as eloping."

"You haven't seen her," Lady Crosby said ominously.

"No, but I had better see Adam, I suppose. I'll write him a letter and you can send a servant round to Berkeley Square with it." He heaved himself to his feet and walked to the door, then turned. "By the way, Ned is getting himself shackled. He's engaged to marry the daughter of a Russian prince."

"A Russian prince!"

"Yes." Lord Dunstanburgh sighed. "I expect it's those long Russian winters. Anyway, he sounds in raptures. The girl's a goddess, according to him, and she is also an heiress. So I suppose it could have been worse." He looked very gloomy.

Lady Crosby was thinking of Stanford. "Yes," she said fervently. "At least she's not already married!"

Stanford and Nanda were at the cottage in Hampstead when Lady Crosby's servant arrived with the Earl of Dunstanburgh's note. At about the time Nanda reached home again, the Duc de Gacé was meeting a French agent in a bookshop in Piccadilly, observed by two men who had been handpicked by Lord Menteith for precisely this task.

After Gacé had passed his book to Bellay, he calmly left the bookstore and proceeded home. He took his wife driving in the park.

Stanford arrived at Berkeley Square at about six o'clock to be greeted with the message from his father. He left immediately for the Crosbys' house in Grosvenor Square.

Chapter 18

What should we speak of
When we are old as you? When we shall hear
The rain and wind beat dark December, how,
In this our pinching cave, shall we discourse
The freezing hours away?

—*Cymbeline*, III, iii, 35-39

Lady Crosby was tactfully absent when Adam Todd was reunited with his father. The earl had been reading a book in one of the smaller saloons, and he put it down when his son came in.

"Papa!" Stanford said, warmth and surprise in his level voice. "How nice to see you! What brings you all the way to London?" He crossed the room and bent to kiss his father's cheek.

The earl waved him to a seat. "You've still a slight limp, I see."

"Yes, but there is no longer any pain. Or at least not much. Dr. Arbuthnot tells me I must resign myself to the limp."

The earl's blue-gray eyes were neutral. "Will you be able to return to the Peninsula?"

"Not, I think, to the job I was doing before. The limp rather slows me up. Besides, I have a strong notion that Napoleon will be finished before the year is out."

There was a brief silence while Lord Dunstanburgh looked at his son. The tired, drawn look Adam had worn when he had left home was gone. He met his father's eyes without reserve, his own densely blue and full of a wry understanding. He knew why his father had come.

Lord Dunstanburgh, faced with the patiently authoritative face of his son, found it difficult to begin. "Ned is engaged," he offered, reaching for the first delaying tactic available.

Stanford smiled delightedly. "Good for him. To his Russian beauty, I suppose."

"You knew about her?" The earl was surprised.

Stanford laughed. "Ned's letters of late have mentioned a certain young lady with revealing regularity." He looked at his father's gloomy face and said, amusement lurking in the corners of his mouth, "I'm quite sure she is civilized, Papa. And she does speak English."

The earl looked up from under his heavy gray brows. "At least she is not married," he said, stealing his sister's line.

There was an ominous silence then Stanford spoke, his voice deceptively pleasant. "Are you referring to me, sir?"

There was something in that voice that set the earl's teeth on edge, but he refused to back down. "I am," he said bluntly.

"I see," said the equable voice of his son. "My Aunt Frances has taken alarm, I gather."

"Yes, she has," returned the earl. "Not to put too fine a point on it, Adam, she has taken a notion that you intend to elope with the Duchesse de Gacé."

"Elope?" There was genuine astonishment on Stanford's face.

"Yes." Lord Dunstanburgh looked at him hopefully. "Of course, Frances has always been prone to exaggerate, but still I thought I'd better come and see what she was getting herself into such a coil about. I see, however, that she was mistaken."

"Yes," said Stanford briefly, his blue eyes like flint, "she was mistaken."

"Good—" the earl was beginning when the cold voice of his son cut him off."

"I am going to marry the duchesse," Stanford said precisely.

"Marry?" The earl was thrown off balance.

"Yes. You may tell my Aunt Frances that much as I might like to elope with Nanda she would hardly consent to elope with me. She has remained in a deeply unhappy marriage for five years for the sake of two children, whom she loves. She would never abandon them to elope with me. Nor will she marry me unless I can arrange it so that upon her divorce from Gacé she is named guardian of the children." He stopped, conscious that his anger had betrayed him into saying too much.

But the earl had heard only one thing. "Divorce!" he said. "Adam, you are not to marry a divorced woman."

No feature of Stanford's face moved, but Lord Dunstanburgh could see the muscles tense beneath the finely textured skin. "Would you prefer me to marry no one, then, Papa? For if I don't marry Nanda de Vaudobin, I can assure you I will never marry at all."

"Nonsense," the earl blustered. "Of course you will marry, but someone suitable to your name and your position. Not a divorced woman." The earl looked at Stanford in genuine horror.

At any other time Stanford would have found his father's typical behavior amusing, but at the moment it did not seem at all funny. "What do you plan to do, then, Papa?" he asked softly. "Disown me? Tell me never to darken your doorstep again?"

"Of course not," the earl snapped. "Things won't come to that."

"They might," his son said grimly.

The earl looked at the beautifully planed face of his heir and recognized the look it wore. There was no mercy in Adam's face. If Lord Dunstanburgh refused to accept this woman, his relationship with his son was as good as over. "Does she mean so much to you?" he asked, his voice barely audible.

Stanford's eyes were brilliant. "Yes."

Lord Dunstanburgh made a weary gesture. He had not expected to win anyway. "Very well," he said. He suddenly felt exhausted, physically battered as if he had been fighting. "But I don't think I can bear a vulgar scandal."

"There will be no scandal," Stanford said soberly.

The earl sat up straighter in his chair. "Well, if you can separate a man from his wife and children without a scandal you must be a miracle maker, Adam. Is Gacé agreeable to a divorce?"

"Gacé knows nothing about a divorce, Papa," Stanford said quietly. "And he must not know anything, at least not yet."

"Good God, Adam!" The earl rose to his feet and stumped around the room, coming to a halt before the chair containing his son. "You tell me you plan to marry this woman and next you say her husband has no intention of divorcing her." His eyes narrowed. "If there is a suit and you are named as corespondent, I *will* tell you never to darken my doorstep."

"I said there would be no scandal," Stanford said patiently. "If things fall out as I plan, Gacé will grant Nanda a divorce and the guardianship of the children."

"There are two children involved, you say?"

"Yes. Virginie is Gacé's daughter by a former marriage. She is ten. Marc is Nanda's son. He is four."

The earl pulled on his iron-gray mustache. "From what you say, Adam, the duchesse has no claim to the girl, and there are very few men who will relinquish custody of their heir." He paced to the marble mantelpiece, then back to his chair. With a grunt he lowered himself into it once again, then gazed steadily once more at the quiet face of his son. "She won't have you without the children, eh?"

"No."

"She can't love you all that much, then, my son."

Stanford's smile was its own answer. "It is not a question of love, Papa. It is a question of need."

"How will you feel, being a father to children not your own?"

"I shall like it very much," Stanford said serenely.

Lord Dunstanburgh pulled once more at his mustache. "You still haven't told me how you propose to bring about this bloodless divorce."

"And I do not intend to tell you, sir. Not yet. I can only beg you not to repeat anything I have told you. Especially not to my Aunt Frances."

The earl looked thoughtfully at his son. "All right, Adam. I'll keep it quiet. And I'll engage to pacify your aunt in some fashion or other." There was a brief pause, then he said slowly, "I understand the duchesse is very beautiful."

Stanford rose to his feet. "I'll bring her around to see you, sir. You will be surprised." He rose and went once again to kiss his father's cheek. "Thank you, Papa," he said, his eyes very blue.

The earl watched as Stanford left the room, a look of ironic resignation in his blue-gray eyes. "What choice did you leave me, my son?" he murmured to the unreceptive air. Then, with a perceptible brightening, he added, "And, after all, the whole enterprise may fail."

When Stanford arrived back at Gacé House for the second time that day he found yet another message awaiting him. Or, to be precise, he found a messenger. He recognized the Menteith livery immediately. "My lord!" said the servant in obvious relief. "I was just about to leave for Crosby House to find you. I have a message to you from Lord Menteith. He charged me strictly to deliver it to your hand myself."

Stanford stretched out his hand in silence and received the note. He read it, folded it, and put it in breast pocket. "Lord Menteith is at home?" he asked the footman.

"Yes, my lord."

"I'm on my way," said Stanford briefly and went off to the stable to tell them not to unharness the bays he had been driving. He swung smoothly into the seat of the phaeton and drove expertly out of the yard, no hint in his driving of the apprehension in his mind.

"It has gone wrong," Menteith had written starkly. "Come at once."

The butler who answered the door at Menteith House in Hanover Square had obviously been expecting him. "This way, my lord," he said as he took Stanford's many-caped driving coat. "Lord Menteith is in the library."

Menteith was alone when Stanford opened the library door. The earl was standing by the window, and his ruffled hair showed the extent of his anxiety. "Stanford! Thank God you are here," he greeted the viscount in fervent tones.

"What has happened, Menteith?" Stanford said as he closed the door carefully behind him. "Where is Bellay?"

"Bellay is dead," Menteith said brutally.

Stanford walked farther into the room, a slight frown the only sign about him that all was not well. There was a moment's silence, then Stanford seated himself in a green-striped wing chair. "You had better tell me the whole," he said quietly.

Menteith came to stand before the fire, his eyes fixed on the composed face of Adam Todd. "It all seemed to be going as you predicted," he began as requested. "Gacé took the memorandum from your desk, as you said he would. And he met Bellay in Fawley's Bookshop, as he had done before."

"Your men were watching him?"

"Yes. Bellay was already in the store when Gacé entered. Gacé picked up a copy of *Reflections upon the French Revolution*, looked through it, then put it back. He finally bought another book and left."

"And Bellay bought the copy of Burke?"

"Yes." Menteith thrust his hand once more through his hair. "That was when things started to go wrong."

Stanford said nothing, merely raised his brows in patient inquiry.

"My men followed Bellay, as instructed," Menteith plodded on. "He had a chaise and four horses waiting for him and headed directly out of London, on the Dover Road."

"Don't tell me your men lost him," Stanford said incredulously.

"No, Stanford. Or at least not in the way you mean," Menteith answered, his voice grim. "They followed Bellay, all right. They didn't want to stop him until they were out of London and on the open road where they would be unobserved."

"And?"

"Someone else had the same idea. Bellay's coach was surprised by highwaymen and Bellay was shot dead in the struggle."

"Highwaymen." Stanford looked very bleak. "Did your men capture these highwaymen?"

"No. And there is worse to come, Stanford. The memorandum was not on Bellay's body."

Stanford's open eyes, gazing steadily at Lord Menteith, looked cold and alien. "What did you find?" he asked evenly.

"A compendium of information, most of which would be of interest to the French. The letter appears to have been written by Denham."

Stanford's vocabulary was always extensive when he was angry. He cursed fluently for some time as he propelled himself out of his chair and paced around the room. Finally he came to rest in front of Menteith.

"I told you he was clever," he said flatly, the passion he had just vented seemingly banished. "We have been a little late, it seems, in making our move."

"What are you talking about, Stanford?"

"Evidently Gacé has decided that England might prove to be uncomfortable for him. He is probably planning to move to the Continent, where he can pass the memorandum along himself. And he has kindly provided us with the name of the traitor we have been so diligently searching for."

"Denham?" Menteith said slowly.

"Denham."

Distractedly the earl thrust his hand through his hair. "We have to get that memorandum back, Stanford," he said urgently. "If you think he means to flee the country . . ."

"I haven't a doubt of it," Stanford said grimly. "Although he will depart perfectly respectably, I am sure, with wife and children in tow."

"But how will he do that?" Menteith's voice was sharp with alarm.

"Oh, he will think of a good reason, our clever duc. There is at least one good thing that has come of this night's work, Menteith."

"And what is that?" the earl asked, uncharacteristic sarcasm in his deep voice.

"He has untied my hands," Stanford answered cryptically.

"I don't understand you, Stanford. We are in the same boat we were in before this grand plan of yours. Only now we are missing a very important memorandum."

Stanford's eyes were blue slits in the stillness of his face. "His grace has just been a bit too clever, Menteith. I never was completely satisfied with our previous plan. Now I can improve upon it."

As he watched the ruthless intensity in Stanford's face, Menteith felt briefly sorry for his traitorous brother-in-law. "Do you mean to tell me what you have in mind?" he inquired after a pause that went on for several minutes.

"No." Stanford smiled at him for the first time that afternoon. "I need time to think about this." Briefly his hand touched Menteith's shoulder. "Don't worry, Robert," he said, his voice now perfectly sober. "I shall deal with Gacé."

Chapter 19

To lapse in fullness
Is sorer than to lie for need, and falsehood
Is worse in kings than beggars. My dear lord,
Thou are one o' the false ones.

—*Cymbeline*, III, vi, 12-15

Nanda was seated at her dressing table, having her hair dressed before leaving for Almack's, when a knock came at the door and Gacé entered. "I should like to speak to you for a few moment, Nanda," he said gravely and looked at her dresser.

"Of course, Matthieu," Nanda responded. "I will call when I want you, Howes," she said to the dresser, who nodded regally and departed.

Nanda turned gracefully around in her seat to face Gacé. "What is it you wish to say to me, Matthieu?" she inquired.

He watched her, gravity in his eyes as well as his voice. In the last few weeks Nanda's beauty had, if possible, become even richer, and the woman Gacé saw facing him glowed with an inner fire that was almost palpable. It was a physical pleasure just to look at her.

Nanda's dark eyes, warmly complemented by her apricot silk dress, looked questioningly at her husband. "I have decided to remove to Baden," he told her calmly. "I should like you and the children to be ready to leave in three days' time."

The beautiful color drained from Nanda's cheeks. "What are you saying, Matthieu?" she whispered.

"I had thought I was perfectly clear. We—that is, you and I and the children—are leaving England in three days' time. We will go to Baden, to Niederwald Castle, and from there to Heidelberg to join the court of Grand Duke Carl."

Her lips were now as pale as her cheeks. "But why, Matthieu?"

"I consider the children are becoming too anglicized," he answered. "It will be as well for them to realize that their heritage does not come from England."

Suddenly the color came back to Nanda's face and her eyes began to sparkle. "For heaven's sake, Matthieu, this is hardly the time to teach the children lessons of that sort! The Continent is extremely unsettled at present. Surely you can wait another year or so, until Napoleon has been beaten and things are normal once more."

"I might, of course, be able to do that, if the children were my sole motive for wishing to leave England." He spoke gravely, almost gently.

The tone of Gacé's voice had subtly altered. The note of gentleness made her careful; she said nothing and he went on. "I think it wise, as well, for you to—ah—leave the country for a few months, *ma belle*. It will benefit us all."

Nanda's heart began to pound, but she managed to speak with the semblance of calm. "I don't know what you are talking about, Matthieu."

"Don't you, *ma belle*?" he said silkily. "Then I will merely say that I take our marriage seriously; you appear to have found a way of not doing so."

"I am afraid I don't understand you," she breathed.

"I think you do." He walked to the window and looked on at the darkened square. "You are having an affair with Lord Stanford," he said calmly. "Perhaps you thought I would look with complaisance upon your actions? Well, I tell you now, I do not. I dislike from the bottom of my heart what you are doing. It's dishonorable; it's indelicate; it's indecent." He turned now to look at her directly. "I do not expect the mother of my children to conduct herself in such a fashion. You will leave for Baden with me, or . . ." He hesitated.

."Or?" she said quietly.

"Or I shall have to take steps to remove the children from your influence."

She stared at him, despair in her heart. He meant it, she thought, as she saw the rigid look about his mouth. He didn't really care about her; it was the appearance of the thing that mattered to him. In that sense, he did take their marriage seriously. It came over her that when he had said that he was after all sincere.

She met his cool gray eyes, her face colorless in the lamplight. "Very well, Matthieu," she said, low. "I will accompany you to Baden."

His expression never changed. "I thought you would see things my way, *ma belle.* We will leave in three days' time." He walked to the door and turned to look once more at her stricken face. "Tell him goodbye, Nanda," he said. "It is finished."

As the door closed behind him she slowly turned around to face the dressing table once again. She put her head down on its polished surface. Then, slowly, deeply, primitively, she began to cry.

By the morning Nanda's passionate grief had expended itself. She felt as if a cold dark mist encompassed her soul. Her love for Stanford had been channeled by the blight of Gacé's touch into the familiar path of renunciation. She braced herself to face Stanford and to tell him.

She was up early, having slept not at all, and went to the morning parlor. "Ask Lord Stanford to come to me here after he has breakfasted," she told a footman. She waited for half an hour before he appeared in the doorway of the room.

"You wanted to see me, Nanda?" he said quietly.

"Yes. Come in, Adam." She looked past him into the hallway. "Close the door for his lordship, James," she said levelly. "We do not wish to be disturbed."

"Yes, your grace." The liveried servant closed the door gently, leaving Nanda and Stanford facing each other across the room. "It really doesn't matter anymore," she said flatly, in answer to his raised brows. "Matthieu knows."

She stood in a blaze of sunlight from the window, and on her face he could clearly see the shadows of sleeplessness. He came into the room until he stood before her. She thought suddenly that he did not look as if he had slept at all either. "What did he say to you?" he asked gently.

She made a hopeless gesture. "That he knows about us. That he won't tolerate our . . . relationship." She spoke as if through an obstruction in her throat. She turned from him suddenly, unable to meet the brilliant blue of his eyes. "We are leaving the country," she said stiffly. "In three days' time. We go to Baden."

Stanford let his breath out slowly. "The clever bastard," he said, a note of what could have been admiration in his voice. "And I played right into his hand."

Startled, Nanda swung around to face him again. "What are you talking about, Adam?" she said sharply, her eyes wide on his face, so mercilessly clear in the sunlight. There was something bitter and dangerous in his eyes, and instinctively she stepped back.

"Did he threaten you with the children?" he asked, his level voice in startling contrast to the look in his eyes.

"Yes," she answered, and at the haunted look on her face he suddenly swore.

He reached out and grasped her arm. "Sit down, Nanda," he said grimly. "It is time I talked to you honestly about Gacé." He propelled her unresistingly to a gold silk-covered sofa and sat down, drawing her along with him.

"Why do you think your brother sent for me to join the staff at the Horse Guards?" he said to her averted face.

"To help coordinate the spring offensive, I imagined," she responded, still refusing to look at him. He had not removed his hand from her arm when they sat down, and she was conscious of its thin hardness biting into her soft flesh. She made no move to shake him off.

"No, it was not to coordinate the spring campaign," he was saying. "It was to find out who at the Horse Guards was a traitor."

"A traitor!" At that she looked at him, her eyes startled.

"Yes. For months there had been leaks of very secret and important information to the French. Menteith was afraid that details about Wellington's campaign would be leaked as well, so he asked me to take on the job of finding out who was the culprit."

There was fear in her eyes now as they looked at him with painful intensity. "And did you find him?" she whispered.

"Yes." There was a pause, then he said gently, "It is Gacé, Nanda. There is no question of his guilt."

There was a passionate silence, then Nanda said strongly, "You are mistaken. It can't be true." She rose to her feet and went to the window.

"It is true," he said quietly.

Impelled by some quality in that quiet voice, she turned to him again. "I knew something was wrong," she said pleadingly. "But not this!"

He remained where he was on the sofa, only said levelly, "Think, my darling. Why did he invite me here in the first place, if not to pick my brains about Wellington's future plans? Why did he throw you and me together with such determination? And now why is he so anxious to get out of the country?"

There was a blind look in her great, dark eyes. "I told you," she said. "He knows about us."

"Of course he knows about us," he responded impatiently. "And he is using that knowledge, as always, to manipulate you into doing what he wants you to do." He rose from the sofa and went over to the window. "Why Baden, Nanda? Baden is part of the Rhenish Confederation, loyal to Napoleon. Why is the Duc de Gacé venturing into the territory of his enemy? Just to get you away from an unfortunate love affair?"

There was a frown on her forehead as she listened to what he was saying. In her mind she went back over the past few months, adding what she had noticed about Gacé's behavior to what Stanford was telling her. She closed her eyes briefly. She had known something was terribly wrong.

She opened her eyes and looked at his face. There was a pulse beating in his right temple. He looked deathly tired. "You were going to let Matthieu go," she said, acknowledging the truth of what he had told her, "if he would give me a divorce and the children." It was a statement, not a question.

A little color came into his face as he recognized her acknowledgement. "Yes," he said. "Menteith and I had a plan all worked out. But Gacé was too clever, and now he is apparently ready to bolt. With, I might add, a very important memorandum in his possession."

She picked up his hand and kissed it. "Tell me," she said softly.

He put his arms around her and drew her close. With his cheek on her shining hair, he related the story of their plan to entrap Gacé and its outcome.

When he had finished she remained still against him. "You think Matthieu had this Bellay killed?" she asked.

"I am sure of it."

She drew a deep, uneven breath. "The children must never know."

"I'll see to it they don't."

She drew away from him and looked up into his face. "What do you want me to do?" she asked simply.

For a long moment he said nothing, his eyes on her set face. There were bruise-colored shadows under her eyes. "I want you to do nothing," he said. "I will take care of everything."

Her pale lips twitched for a moment, wryly. "Don't try to spare me, my love. Matthieu must be stopped before he passes that memorandum along. I know that."

He smiled at her, and his eyes were very tender. "I will stop him, Nanda. Will you tell me what his travel plans are?"

"Yes."

"Good girl. Let him think you have said goodbye to me. Try to act as normally as possible. It will all be over in a few more weeks."

"You will offer him the same terms as before?"

There was something cold and terrifying in his eyes that she had never seen before. "He will not like the terms I plan to offer him," he said evenly, "but he will have little choice in the matter."

There was an aching tightness in Nanda's throat as she looked at him, but the time had long since passed since she could ask him for mercy. He would never willingly hurt her, of that she was sure. But his first duty lay in silencing Gacé. She swallowed painfully and reached out to touch his arm. "Do whatever you feel you must, Adam," she said soberly. "If it were not for me you would have Matthieu safely arrested. There are too many lives in his grasp now to take any chances on his escaping. Whatever you do, I will understand."

He looked at her slender hand as it lay on his blue-coated arm. His long lashes hid his eyes as he said, "Will you, my darling? I will hold you to that promise, you know." Then he reached out and pulled her into his arms, holding her to him with a desperate strength that nearly crushed her ribs. But she made no protest, merely raised her face to his, wanting the urgency of his mouth against hers to blot out the treacherous darkness that seemed to threaten from all sides.

Chapter 20

... our cage
We make a choir, as doth the prisoned bird,
And sing our bondage freely.
—*Cymbeline*, III, iii, 43-45

Nanda broke the news of their upcoming journey to the children that afternoon. Marc was delighted by the thought of a long trip by sea and took for granted Nanda's explanation that Papa was going on a mission for the king.

Virginie was a different matter. Her memories of Germany were limited, but what she did remember was unhappy. "You are coming with us, Mama?" she asked Nanda several times, and Nanda's reassurance seemed to do little to ease her mind.

"Come with me, darling," Nanda said gently, when she turned around for the eighth time in one hour to find Ginny under her feet. She took the little girl by the hand and led her into the morning parlor. She seated herself on the gold sofa, Ginny's hand still in hers. She turned to look into the hazel eyes of her stepdaughter and said soberly, "I want you to listen to me, Ginny. What I am going to say is very serious."

"Yes, Mama." There was apprehension in Ginny's small voice.

"I have never said this to you, because I thought you knew it, but I will say it now. You are not the child of my body, but you are the child of my heart. There are no circumstances, absolutely none, under which I would consider leaving you." There was no emotion in Nanda's voice, only calm conviction. Ginny's mouth trembled and tears came to her eyes. She threw herself into Nanda's arms and clung tightly.

There were tears in Nanda's eyes as well as she looked down at the silvery head buried in her shoulder, but her voice preserved its calm. Ginny's mother had died in Germany, and that loss was part of what had triggered this fearful reaction. But Nanda did not think the deep-buried memory of her mother's loss was the only factor involved. Virginie was an extremely sensitive child; she had sensed the upheaval in Nanda's own emotions. As she held the slender, quivering body close, murmuring words of comfort, Nanda blamed herself for Ginny's fear.

What she had told Ginny was true: there were no circumstances under which Nanda would abandon her. But, during these last months, her love for the children had, for the first time, begun to be a burden. But for them, she and Adam could be together. But for them, her suffocating marriage could be terminated and she would be free to go to the man she loved. But for them.

During the last months it had seemed as if the children's fingers were on her heartstrings, pulling and tearing at her love and her loyalty. For the first time she had begun to resent them.

But now, holding the light body of her stepdaughter and feeling her grief, that resentment was gone. This trip to Baden was the last move in the game Matthieu and Adam had been playing. Whatever the outcome between the two men, her job was to protect the children. So she kissed Ginny's pale curls and tipped her face up to be dried with Nanda's delicate lace-edged handkerchief.

"I am going to ask Miss Braxton to take you for a walk in the park," she said briskly. "I need a little peace to get this family packed and ready to go by Monday."

A smile trembled on Ginny's lips. "Yes, Mama," she said. She reached out to hug Nanda once again. "I love you," she whispered. She pulled back and looked at Nanda, a heroic light in her eyes. "I will even ride with Marc in the chaise," she said staunchly, "and help keep him out of Papa's way."

Nanda laughed. "Your reward will be in heaven, my darling," she teased. "Come." She rose gracefully to her feet. "Let us go and find Miss Braxton."

While Nanda was organizing her household, Stanford was organizing a move of a very different order. The first thing he did was to make sure Gacé was under surveillance during the entire journey. Nanda had told him they were traveling with Marc's nurse, Ginny's governess, her own dresser, and Gacé's valet. Stanford proceeded to bribe Gacé's valet with a very impressive sum of money to inform his grace that he would not consider leaving England at this point in time. He was, however, to recommend a substitute, and, as Gacé was pressed for time, the substitute was approved.

Gacé's valet did not have to look far to find an explanation for Stanford's behavior. It was no secret in the servants' quarters that Lord Stanford and her grace were having an *affaire du coeur*; it was natural that his lordship would want someone to keep an eye on her husband. The valet, who really did not wish to cross into French territory, was more than pleased to oblige his lordship.

Gacé's new valet had served with Stanford in the Peninsula. "Don't let Gacé out of your sight," Stanford warned him. "I think his contact is probably in Baden, but I don't want to take any chances of his passing along that memorandum during the journey."

"I'll watch him like a hawk, my lord," Lieutenant

George Ross assured Stanford. "But I'm afraid he'll find me a queer sort of a valet."

Stanford shrugged. "You took care of your own clothes in the Peninsula, so you can take care of Gacé for a few weeks. By the time he gets around to sacking you, the game will be over."

Lieutenant Ross looked at the cool face of Lord Stanford and nodded. "Yes, my lord. And how am I to get in touch with you, in case something does happen on the journey?"

"I will be in touch with you," Stanford replied. "They are landing in Stade and driving right to Hanover. From Hanover they go to Kassel, from Kassel to Frankfurt, and from Frankfurt to Niederwald Castle, outside of Mannheim. I will be in touch with you at all stops."

"Yes, my lord." Lieutenant Ross was dressed for his part as a valet, but there was a look of easy competence about him that betrayed the soldier. Stanford was almost sure that Gacé would not make his move until he was at Niederwald, but the inclusion of Ross in the duc's party made him feel a good deal more comfortable. He held out his hand, and the other man clasped it firmly. "We will get that memorandum back, my lord," he said. "I'm sure of it."

"So am I," said Stanford grimly.

In a long conference with Menteith, Stanford set up their plans for entrapping Gacé. As a result of that meeting four men left London for Dover, arriving after midnight, in time to catch the morning tide. Their destination was Gluckstadt in Holstein, whence they were to proceed with all haste to Baden, there to prepare a welcome for the Duc de Gacé.

Stanford also prepared to leave for Germany. As he planned to arrive in Stade as a common sailor and then transform himself into a German merchant, he required several changes of clothes and spent the afternoon shopping.

He also visited his solicitor and had him draw up a will.

Later that evening, after a dinner with Menteith, Stanford called at Crosby House to see his father. Lord Dunstanburgh was preparing to accompany his sister and brother-in-law to a reception, but he excused himself when he saw his son. "I'll join you later, Frances," he said in response to Lady Crosby's protests. "Adam can hardly come with us; he isn't properly dressed."

Lady Crosby looked with hauteur at her nephew's polished boots and beautifully cut coat of blue superfine. It was not correct attire for the evening.

"Sorry, Aunt Frances," Stanford said, the hint of a smile on his firm mouth, "but I really do need to see my father. I won't keep him long."

"Very well, Adam." She sighed wearily. "We shall see you shortly, Richard," and she swept from the room.

Lord Crosby regarded Stanford with the suspicion of a twinkle in his eyes. "Your aunt feels you are letting down the family, I am afraid. But she'll come around, Adam. She always does," and he followed his wife out to the waiting carriage.

Lord Dunstanburgh, correctly attired in knee breeches, black coat, and white waistcoat, seated himself in a tapestried armchair with a winged back. "Now, Adam," he said serenely, "what is it that you have come to see me about?"

"I have come to ask a favor of you, Papa." Stanford spoke through stiff lips.

"What is it?" A slight frown appeared between Lord Dunstanburgh's shaggy brows as he contemplated his son.

"What I have to tell you must not go any further. Ever."

The earl leaned forward slightly. "Sit down, Adam. You can rely on me to keep a still tongue in my head."

Stanford sat down in a rosewood chair, facing his father across a table of inlaid ivory. "It has to do with Nanda," he said carefully. "You asked me before how I planned to get Gacé to give her a divorce and guardianship of the children."

"Yes."

"Well, I was going to blackmail him." The earl's expression never changed as he sat quietly, listening to his son. "You will recall I was sent for originally because of a security problem," Stanford continued. "The problem was that someone at the Horse Guards, someone highly placed, was passing information to the French." Stanford spoke slowly to his father's calm face. "That someone was Gacé."

The earl's voice was noncommittal. "I see. When did you discover this?"

"A few months ago. At about the same time that I fell in love with his wife."

"I see," the earl said again.

"Nanda didn't know, of course. No one did except myself and then Menteith. I persuaded him to go along with a magnificent plan I concocted to convict Gacé, save the family from the scandal of his actions, and free Nanda to marry me." Stanford's hands moved for a moment, restlessly, then were stilled. "I wasn't completely happy with it, but, under the circumstances, it was the best I could come up with."

"And?"

"Oh, Gacé slipped through the trap, slick as a weasel. He is now planning to remove himself, and his family, to Baden."

"You have no proof against him?"

"Nothing that would stand up before the law. And

even if I did, how could I subject Marc and Ginny to the horror of knowing the truth about their father? They don't love him, but his blood, after all, does run in their veins."

Lord Dunstanburgh watched his son and knew it was Adam's own pride of family that caused him to speak in such a way. And his pride in his father, as well. The earl was obscurely moved as he watched the play of emotion on Adam's normally reserved face. "What is your alternative?" he asked quietly.

"There is only one that I can think of, and I hope to God I can pull it off. They leave for Baden on Monday; I am leaving tonight. Whatever else may happen, Gacé must be stopped. He has in his possession a very important secret memorandum." The chiseled face of his son held a look Lord Dunstanburgh had never seen before. Unaccountably, he was suddenly afraid.

"What do you want me to do, Adam?" His voice was harsh with controlled emotion.

"Whatever happens, Papa, is not going to be pleasant for Nanda. We will be coming back by sea, and I should like to bring her to Dunstanburgh Castle, instead of going on to Dover. We can come right into Embleton Bay and be at Dunstanburgh in half an hour. Then we can decide what to do and what to tell her family and friends. I must warn you, sir," Stanford concluded slowly, "that I am hoping she will agree to marry me immediately."

"And what about her husband?" the earl asked this stranger who was also his son.

There was a catastrophic silence as Stanford stared at his father, glittering resistance in his eyes.

"I see," Lord Dunstanburgh said, his voice deathly tired. "Very well, you may bring the duchesse to Dunstanburgh. I will be there."

"Thank you, sir." Stanford rose to his feet and regarded his father's face, a slight frown between his black brows. "It is not her fault, Papa," he said unexpectedly. "She was eighteen when she married him, and she has been loyal to him for five hellish years. She has courage, the kind of courage that not only gives but gives up. She was ready to give up her own happiness because of the needs of two children. It is not just that the innocent should be the only sufferers."

"No," the earl said slowly. "No, I suppose not."

Stanford came to the earl's side and for a moment his long fingers grasped his father's shoulder. Then, without another word, he walked rapidly to the door, his long stride hardly impeded by the limp that was his legacy from Burgos. Lord Dunstanburgh's eyes were deeply troubled as he watched him go.

Chapter 21

I am sorry, Cymbeline,
That I am to pronounce Augustus Caesar—
Caesar, that hath more kings his servants than
Thyself domestic officers—thine enemy. . . .
            —*Cymbeline*, III, 1, 62-65

It was eleven o'clock on Monday morning when the Duc de Gacé and his family left for Dover to board the yacht the duc had hired for this momentous journey. In the Gacé traveling coach rode the duc and the duchesse, the ducal crest on the door informing any interested parties of their rank. The four shining black horses were driven by the Gacé coachman, who was accompanied on the seat by a footman. Behind the ducal carriage came a coach carrying Marc and Ginny, Marc's nurse, and Ginny's governess. The last coach in the procession bore Gacé's valet, Nanda's dresser, and mounds of luggage.

They stopped at Rochester to change horses and have something to eat. The children were in good spirits, both keyed up at the thought of their coming sea journey. Ginny expatiated at great length about her freedom from sickness on her last trip by sea, which she remembered not at all, being all of three years old at the time. Gacé finally said, "My dear Virginie, if you mention one more word on this repulsive subject I shall ask you to await us in the coach. It is hardly a topic for the luncheon table."

Ginny flushed and subsided, flashing a look at Nanda.

"Your father is right, darling," Nanda said firmly. "Let us choose a more pleasant topic for discussion."

"I believe, Nanda—" Gacé was beginning when Marc cut in.

"Can I help steer the boat?" he asked, excitedly drumming his heels against his chair. "Ginny says I'm too small, but I'm not! I'm four years old, Mama." He reached out to grasp Nanda's arm and knocked over a glass of wine.

Wordlessly Gacé got to his feet and left the table.

"I didn't mean it, Mama," Marc cried anxiously. "It was an accident, Mama."

"I know it was an accident, Marc," Nanda said resignedly, as she moved Marc aside to let the servant clean up. "It is quite all right," she told the fussing innkeeper. "No, please don't change the linen. We are finished, I assure you." Then, as Marc was still pulling at her arm, she turned to him in exasperation. "What *is* it, Marc?"

His lip quivered and his dark eyes brimmed. "You yelled at me," he said reproachfully.

She took a firm grip on her temper and shook her head at Miss Fergus, who had stepped forward to claim Marc. "I know you are excited, darling, but you must try to be more careful. And try not to talk so much when Papa is around. He is not used to dining with small children, remember. He likes a little peace with his meals."

Both Marc and Ginny looked at their mother's anxious face and nodded solemnly. With the unfailing instinct of the young they had always known they must do what they could to protect their mother against their father. "Yes, Mama," they chorused.

"Good." She turned to leave the inn and behind her heard Marc saying, "I'm going to steer a little bit, Fergie. Not all the time. Just almost." She heaved a weary sigh and went to join Gacé where he stood beside the traveling coach, a thin line between his brows. After a journey of several weeks in close proximity to his children, he might well be glad to hand them over to her permanently, she thought, with the first gleam of humor she had felt in days.

They arrived in Dover in time for dinner. Gacé had hired a private parlor at the King's Inn, and, since they could hardly ask the children to eat in the crowded dining room alone, they dined *en famille* once again.

Aside from one or two heated interchanges between them, dealing with the nature of Marc's appetite, dinner was relatively peaceful. Both children were on their best behavior, and they were hungry, which kept them occupied. Nanda determinedly kept up a flow of light conversation which she addressed mainly to her husband.

Marc put down his fork and sighed gustily. "I was a hungry boy," he told Nanda. He got off his chair. "Now I have to go relieve myself," he announced to the table at large.

There was a white line around Gacé's mouth. "Good God, Nanda," he said to his wife. "The child has no more manners than a barbarian. Is this your idea of child-rearing?"

Marc looked interested. "What is a barbarian, Papa?"

"A barbarian is someone who ought not to be allowed in civilized company," his father told him blightingly.

Marc frowned in bewilderment, but his physical needs were more pressing. "I have to . . ." he began to wail, when Nanda grabbed him by the shoulder.

"Go upstairs, Marc," she said hastily. "Fergie is there. Have her dress you for bed. I'll come along to tuck you in."

"But I want—" her recalcitrant son was beginning, when Gacé said in the cold voice Marc feared more than his mother's heated anger, "Go."

Marc went. "He is very tired, Matthieu," Nanda said placatingly. "It was a long day for such a little boy."

"He was very good in the coach, Papa," Ginny offered helpfully, then fell silent at her father's look. They finished the meal in the same silence, and Nanda excused herself with Ginny. "I'll just run along to see how Marc is doing," she said lightly.

He was almost asleep, looking very small in the big bed. He stirred sleepily when she bent to kiss him. "Are you angry, Mama?" he murmured.

"No, darling, I'm not angry."

"I didn't mean it."

Reluctantly, Nanda smiled. "They ought to write that on your coat-of-arms, Marc," she said. "Goodnight, my love."

She went straight to her room instead of returning downstairs. She didn't trust herself to see Gacé again. She was angry, but not with Marc. She soaked in the luxury of a hot bath, donned a fresh lawn nightgown, and let Howes brush and plait her hair. "Thank you, Howes," she said gently. "You must be tired as well. Go to bed. We are leaving on the early tide."

"Yes, your grace." The woman nodded in her stately fashion and went to the door, almost colliding with Gacé, who had his hand raised to knock.

"Excuse me, your grace," she murmured and went, leaving Gacé to enter and close the door behind him.

He stood for a minute looking at his wife. Her dark hair was pulled loosely off her face and fell in a shining plait between her shoulders. She stood in front of the fire, and the lines of her body were visible through the thin lawn of her nightdress.

"I thought you were coming back downstairs again," he said.

"I am very tired," she answered in her low, vibrant voice. "I decided to go right to bed."

"Marc and Virginie would wear anyone out," he agreed.

As she stared at his finely modeled, sensitive face the anger she had been repressing surfaced. "You only had two meals with them," she said. "It's the most time you've spent in their company in years."

He raised an eyebrow. "And whose fault is that?" he inquired. "I would be perfectly willing to spend more time with my children if they behaved according to my wishes, not as English versions of Attila the Hun."

Warm color stained her cheeks. "Children aren't small adults, Matthieu. It isn't natural that they be made to behave as if they were."

"Perhaps not. But they certainly should be made to behave. Marc is appallingly undisciplined, Nanda."

The color in her cheeks deepened. She knew Marc lacked the discipline a man could give him, but it was impossible to explain to Gacé that his cold, blighting manner was profoundly harmful to a warm, loving child. Marc responded very well to the guidance of her brother, and of Adam too, she thought. His father inspired rebellion in him, not obedience. She shook her head. "We've been through all this before," she said.

"Yes, we have," he returned smoothly. "And I allowed you the freedom to rear my children in whatever fashion you felt best. But you must not expect me to praise the result."

"I don't," she said shortly.

He leisurely crossed the room until he was standing before her. "Do you also remember that you agreed to conform to my idea of what a wife should be?"

"Yes," she said, through a suddenly constricted throat.

"You have not exactly done that, *ma belle*, have you?" He tipped her chin up so she was forced to look at him. At the expression on his face, her blood seemed to run cold. She knew now why he had come to her room.

"I have tried, Matthieu," she said breathlessly. "I agreed to come to Baden with you. But you must give me time."

"Time?" His gray eyes were narrow. "We have been

married for five years, *ma belle*. I am hardly a stranger to you."

Yes, you are, she thought suddenly, and the thought gave her courage. This was not Matthieu, her stiff, proud husband who could not help it if he lived in a world of restrictions that suffocated and withered her soul. This was a man who was ready to betray the nation and the people who had befriended him; to betray as well the trust and the fellowship of his own people, who believed him their ally, indeed, their guide. There was neither love nor loyalty in him; only a monstrous egotism that saw others merely as objects to be used for its own glorification. Her spine stiffened. No matter what happened, he should never touch her again.

Her position at the moment, she realized, was weak. Excellent chess player that she was, Nanda went on the offensive. "As for that, Matthieu," she said, raising her eyebrows, "You have hardly been a pattern of fidelity yourself, have you?"

He looked surprised. "That is not the same thing."

"Not to you, certainly," she agreed, "but you can hardly think I enjoyed knowing you spent your time with Lady Bellerman or with that red-headed dancer from the opera."

She had never before, by the slightest hint, betrayed that she knew about his affairs. There was a pinched look about his nostrils. "Those women have nothing to do with you," he said.

"Of course not," she said nastily. "After all, you take our marriage seriously and I do not."

"You are being ridiculous," he said stiffly.

"I don't think so." She dashed angry tears from her eyes. "The only thing that holds our marriage together, Matthieu, are two children, and don't presume too much on them."

"Are you saying you refuse to act as my wife ever again?"

She saw the temper in his eyes and felt it prudent to temporize. Stanford's words sounded again in her mind; try to act as normally as possible. Normally, she would never defy Matthieu like this. He held the hostages. She raised her chin and looked straight into his eyes. "No, I am not saying that, Matthieu. I am saying that you must give me time, time to . . . accustom myself."

There was a tense silence as they stared at each other, then the danger seemed to fade from Gacé's eyes. "Very well, Nanda," he said. "I won't press you—for the moment." He walked to the door and turned at its threshold to address her again. "You are the only woman who is important to me, *ma belle*. Remember that."

Nanda got into bed, her full lips thin with distaste. She pulled the covers up over her head and repeated a few satisfying swear words she had learned from Stanford. Then she went to sleep.

The yacht they boarded the next morning had several comfortable, large cabins, and Nanda had one to herself. They sailed out of Dover on the ten-o'clock tide, heading north to circle Holland, now part of the French Empire, and sail up the Elbe River to disembark at Stade. The port of Stade was also in French territory, but Gacé planned to leave immediately and drive through till they were in Hanover, which was part of the Confederation of the Rhine.

As the yacht sailed out of Dover, Nanda stood on deck with the two children beside her. Stanford, she knew, had already sailed, his destination the same as hers. Her knuckles were white on the rail as she watched the water grow between the yacht and the shore. She put an arm around either child and hugged them convulsively. Then she went below to help supervise the unpacking.

Chapter 22

... those that are betrayed
Do feel the treason sharply, yet the traitor
Stands in worse case of woe.
—*Cymbeline*, III, iv, 87-89

Stanford arrived in Stade a full day before the Gacé yacht. He landed as a crew member of a small boat carrying wood and disappeared almost instantly into the town. The men he had sent on ahead of him were landing at Gluckstadt, in Holstein, and had orders to proceed directly to Mannheim, the city close to Niederwald, Gacé's estate on the east bank of the Rhine. The east bank was part of Baden; on the other side of the river lay the French Empire, and it was at Niederwald that Stanford was sure the conclusion of the drama would be played out.

Stanford himself, to make assurance doubly sure, was planning to follow Gacé as he moved south through Westphalia and Frankfurt to Baden. At each evening's stop he would make contact with Lieutenant Ross. He also planned to make arrangements along the way for a speedy return trip to Stade, should it prove necessary.

The Gacé yacht arrived in the Stade channel early the following morning, and the party disembarked with little trouble. They breakfasted at the local inn, and by that time their carriages were unloaded from the yacht. Horses had been hired in the town by the efficient Ross and the family and servants were ready to leave. Nanda marveled, as they passed through the green, flat Altes

Land, that the country could look so peaceful. War seemed very far away. She glanced at Gacé's profile as he sat beside her in the swaying coach. The war, she realized suddenly, was in fact never closer.

They arrived at Niederwald Castle, where Virginie had been born and where her mother was buried, five days later. At Kassel and at Frankfurt they had stayed with friends of Gacé's, and by the time they arrived at the long yellow eighteenth-century castle with its vineyards and view of the Rheingau hills, Nanda was exhausted with the constant strain of dissimulation and surveillance. She had learned to school her face and hide her feelings long ago, but the knowledge of that memorandum in Gacé's keeping had her nerves on edge. Between her and Ross they had managed to keep Gacé under constant watch; he had made no effort to be alone with any of his hosts.

She had thought she could relax a little at Niederwald, but in fact her tension only grew. The children were thrilled to finally stop traveling; five days cooped up in a coach had tried them severely. The castle was only five miles from the Rhine, and Nanda took them to the river for an excursion and picnic two days after they arrived. As they laughed and explored, she had stood staring across the river to the opposite bank, which lay within the French Empire. It was just south of here, at Ettenheim on the Rhine, that Napoleon had kidnapped Ginny's uncle, the Duc d'Enghien, nine years before. The young man, the Prince de Condé's only son, had been brought to Paris, tried, and shot ninety minutes after the trial was over.

Nanda thought of Adam, hidden somewhere in the vicinity, and shivered although the day was warm. Calling to the children to pick up their things, she returned to the castle and did not herself go back to the Rhine.

Stanford was in fact about eight miles away in an abandoned hut he had discovered in the Rheingau hills. He had met up with Menteith's four men in Mannheim, and together they took on the task of keeping the Duc de Gacé under constant watch. This entailed a continual surveillance of the Mannheim-Heidelberg road outside of Niederwald, as well as a personal guard on Gacé himself.

The watch on Gacé was left to Ross and to Smith, whose father's real name had been Schmidt and who spoke fluent German as a result. He had managed to get taken on in the stables at Niederwald, as the arrival of the duc and the duchesse put a burden on the limited staff. Stanford and the other three watched the roads.

It was a week before Gacé made his move, and they were all heartily sick of hours of crouching motionless behind bushes, with their horses tied up at a convenient distance. "I won't be dining home tonight, *ma belle*," Gacé told Nanda at lunch. "I am going into Mannheim on some business and I shall dine there with friends."

Nanda's voice was steady enough, although her heart had begun to pound. "Very well, Matthieu. Will you be late?"

"Not too late, I think. But don't have anyone wait up for me. I will let myself in."

"Very well," she said again, hoping he would not notice her suddenly uneven breathing.

He left the house at about six o'clock, dressed in buckskins and polished boots; he was riding. Nanda watched him from the window of her bedroom as he rode down the drive, tall and elegant in the saddle of his gray horse. Three minutes later Ross also left the house to race to the stables. There he explained in French to the bewildered grooms that monseigneur had forgotten a paper of vast importance and he, Ross, must catch him up to give it to him.

Schmidt was the only stablehand to speak French, and he quickly produced a horse for Herr Ross, enabling the valet to follow his master immediately. Ross left him explaining in German to the other grooms exactly what it was Herr Ross had said.

Ensigns Anderson and Lowry were on duty when Gacé rode down the Niederwald road and headed toward Mannheim. Ensign Anderson was on the Mannheim side, and when he saw Gacé ride past he heaved a great sigh of thankfulness. He went for his horse and, as soon as Gacé was far enough down the road, he started after him.

Five minutes later Lieutenant Ross came galloping to the place where he knew the sentry for the Heidelberg side of the road should be hidden. Ensign Lowry joined him immediately on the road. "This is it, I think," Lieutenant Ross said tersely. "He's going toward Mannheim." Within a few minutes they had caught up to Ensign Anderson.

Gacé continued along the road for about five miles, then veered off on a narrow road heading toward the river. The road led to the ruins of Hattenheim, an ancient feudal castle that was now no more than a heap of stone with two crumbling towers. Gacé tethered his horse and walked to the ruins, which gave a commanding view of the Rhine. As he approached the castle, a man stepped from the shadow of one of the towers. "Monsiegneur de Gacé?" he said.

Gacé joined him and the two men stood for a few minutes in quiet conversation. Then Gacé took a paper from his breast pocket and handed it to the Frenchman. They spoke for a minute longer, then both men moved to return to their horses.

Gacé's horse was not there.

With an oath on his lips he turned to look for the Frenchman only to find himself facing his valet and the point of a gun. "I have your horse, your grace," Ross said pleasantly. "Don't try to run for it, please. You would not get far."

There was a shout from the other side of the ruins, then the sound of a shot. Ross' gun never wavered, nor did his eyes leave Gacé. A man came running across the rocky grass. "I'm sorry, lieutenant, but the fool tried to run."

"Did you get the memorandum?" Ross asked tersely.

"Yes, lieutenant. I have it here."

Ross didn't even glance at the paper Ensign Anderson held up. The look on Gacé's face told him all he needed to know. "Is the Frenchman dead?" he asked.

"Yes, lieutenant," the ensign said again.

Ross frowned. "Tie him on his horse. We don't want him to be found too quickly. We'll take him back with us to the hut." He motioned with his gun. "You are coming with us too, your grace. My lord is most anxious to see you."

Slowly Gacé moved toward where Lieutenant Ross had pointed. He said nothing. The English voices, the use of military titles, their knowledge of the memorandum, all told him more than enough. With his mouth set in a bitter line he mounted his horse, conscious of the guns in the hands of the three men surrounding him. Ross was right; he would not get far if he ran. He would wait until he met "my lord." Perhaps there was still a chance of salvaging something out of this debacle.

They arrived at the hut some forty minutes later, having veered off the main road and into the hills immediately. The setting sun was behind them as they stopped in front of a rough, wooden hut with a man sitting outside the door. Ensign Castleton rose to his feet, his lips pursed in a soundless whistle. "Will my lord be glad to see you!" he said to Lieutenant Ross.

"Where is he?" asked Ross.

Ensign Castleton gestured toward the hut. "Inside."

"Wait here," Ross said to the others. As Gacé dismounted from his horse, Ross entered the hut.

"Did you get the paper?" Castleton asked Ensign Anderson.

"Yes. Ross has it."

There was silence as three pairs of hostile eyes watched Gacé, then Ross came out. "You can go inside, now," Ross said to the duc. "My lord wants to see you."

Gacé's face was impassive as he walked to the door and bent his tall head to enter the hut. The room was dim after the outside, lit only by a tiny window and a single candle. The candle stood on a makeshift table, behind which sat a man. As he took in the face reflected in the glow of the candle, Gacé drew a sharp, hissing breath. "Stanford!" He sounded profoundly shaken.

"Come in, Gacé," Stanford said, his voice expressionless.

The duc took two more steps into the room, then stopped. "How did you get here?" he asked harshly.

Stanford's face in the glow of the candle was a shuttered mask. "The same way you did," he returned. "I really could not allow you to pass along that memorandum."

There was a shocked silence, then Gacé came a little farther into the room. "It was a trap," he said slowly. "You let me take it."

The candle lit Stanford's face from underneath, making it look remote and stern. "I let you take it," he agreed. "I had been aware of your guilt for quite some time, but I needed proof. Your disposal of Bellay forced us to take the rather exotic measures of today."

There was a pinched look about Gacé's mouth and nostrils. "Who else knows besides you?" he asked tensely.

"The men who are here today. Menteith." There was a pause. "Nanda."

"Nanda!" Gacé took an uneven breath. "It was not

wise of me to have invited you to stay with us, was it, Stanford?" he asked finally, with an effort at his old irony.

"No. It was not very wise of you."

Gacé came one step closer to the table. Stanford's hands, empty, lay on the table before him, next to a neat pile of papers. "What are you going to do?" Gacé asked the carefully guarded face of Adam Todd.

"I should kill you," Stanford returned pleasantly, "but I won't. I am going to take you back to England, Gacé, to stand trial."

"No!" Sheer panic sounded in Gacé's light, precise voice. "Nanda would never forgive you if you did that, Stanford. The scandal would ruin her. And my children." With desperate urgency he begged, "Let me go."

With a movement of unexpected violence, Stanford pushed back his chair and rose. "I wish I could, Gacé. I don't relish the prospect of putting your family through a national scandal either. If we had caught you in England, perhaps we might have arranged something. But not now. You know what is in that memorandum."

"I won't betray you."

Stanford said nothing, but there was a distinctly sardonic look in his blue eyes. Gacé's own eyes fell before that look. He moistened his lips. "Marc and Virginie will be disgraced for life," he said with difficulty. "My name will be destroyed."

There was bitter anger in Stanford's voice. "You should have thought of that before you turned spy, Gacé."

The duc stared at the man standing now some six feet from him. For a long moment their eyes held, and Gacé correctly read the expression in Stanford's brilliant gaze. He said softly, "Then kill me, Stanford. You want to."

There was a tense pause, then Stanford said in his ordinary voice, as though he were refusing an invitation to dine, "I can't."

"Why not?"

"Because of Nanda, of course. She would always wonder if she were the reason I did it."

There was a trace of bitterness in Gacé's voice. "Do you think she would mourn my death?"

"No," returned Stanford with brutal honesty. "But she would hate being the reason for my committing a murder."

Gacé looked into the dark face of the other man and knew that if it were not for Nanda, Stanford would have killed him without pity. He wet his lips and tried again. "She will hate even more seeing me tried for treason. She will never forgive you for the disgrace you will bring on the children."

"I can't," Stanford said again, finally.

"God, Stanford," Gacé said, his voice cracking, "don't do this to me. They will hang me, do you realize that?"

The hills outside were dimming toward night; the room now was lit only by the single candle. Stanford leaned back against the wooden wall of the hut and bent his head to study the dirt floor at his feet. "Of course," he said calmly, "there is another way."

Gacé's head jerked slightly. "And what is that?"

Head still bent, Stanford said evenly, "I might lend you a gun."

For a moment Gacé did not understand him, then Stanford raised his head. There was about his whole figure, as he leaned against the wall of the abandoned hut, a dark and icy detachment that, more than anything else, gave Gacé his meaning.

The duc waited a moment, until he was sure his voice was under control. He finally said carefully, "What else would you do, if you lent me a gun?"

Stanford went back to the table and placed his hand on the papers piled neatly in the center. Gacé's eyes were riveted to that strong, thin hand, outlined so clearly by the candle. "I would see to it that your reputation remained cloudless," Stanford said equably. "I will give it out you were on a mission for the War Department. Your son and daughter will never know the truth. You will be a hero, Gacé."

The duc's eyes remained on Stanford's hand. "And what do you want?" he asked. "Besides, of course, my wife."

A muscle tightened in Stanford's jaw but he answered evenly, "I want you to sign this." He picked up the papers and extended them toward the duc.

Gacé took them, hesitated a moment, but the rock of Stanford's face told him nothing. His face set as he bent his head to look at the papers he held. With a profound shock, he realized he was holding his own will. He looked up sharply to Stanford, but the viscount's face was as granitelike as before. "Read it," he said, his voice expressionless.

Gacé did. It was clear and straightforward, bequeathing all of his English and French property to Marc together with a handsome dowry for Ginny, as well as Niederwald Castle. For Nanda there was only the amount of her own dowry, as well as the guardianship of both children.

There was a long silence, then Gacé took a deep breath. "Very well," he said.

Silently Stanford went to the door and called in Lieutenant Ross and Ensign Castleton. Gacé signed his name and the two soldiers signed as witnesses. They left.

"For how long have you planned this?" Gacé asked, his voice quite steady.

"Since the day I heard you were coming to Baden."

"*Eh bien.*" Gacé made a small gesture of defeat. "Give me the gun."

Stanford drew a small revolver from his breast pocket and placed it on the table. "It has one bullet in it," he said, and walked to the door. He did not look back.

The men outside seemed surprised to see him. "What

should we do with the Frenchman, my lord?" asked Ross.

"Bury him. Then head back for Holstein."

"But what about the duc?" Ensign Anderson was beginning when there was the sound of a shot from within the hut.

"I believe Gacé has solved that problem for us," Stanford said, his voice perfectly neutral. "I will return his body to Niederwald for burial."

Chapter 23

Oh, for a horse with wings!
—*Cymbeline*, III, ii, 50

It was quite dark by the time Stanford rode into the courtyard of Niederwald Castle with the dead body of Gacé tied to the horse he was leading. The duc had shot himself directly through the heart.

Stanford gave instructions to the majordomo who had come out to meet him, then entered the house himself. Nanda, he had been told, was upstairs in the family sitting room.

She met him on the stairs. "Adam!" She was white to the lips. "What happened? I saw you ride in. Is Matthieu . . ." She paused, her eyes filled with painful anxiety.

"Come into the sitting room," he said firmly. "I cannot talk to you in the hallway."

Obediently she turned and preceded him back up the stairs to the room she had just run out of. He closed the door firmly behind them and looked at her gravely.

"Gacé is dead," he said quietly. "He shot himself."

What little color there was in her face fled. "Shot himself?" she whispered. "But how?"

"He asked me for a gun," Stanford said, somewhat mendaciously, "and I gave him one."

She swayed a little and he reached out to steady her. "Sit down, Nanda," he said, guiding her to a chair.

"I'm all right," she said faintly, sitting gratefully on a tapestried sofa. Stanford glanced around the room and saw the decanters set up on the corner table. He went over and poured something in a glass and brought it back to her.

It was brandy. She sipped, choked a little, but the color came back to her face. "You had better tell me what happened," she said in a stronger voice.

He sat down beside her and began to talk. What he told her was substantially the truth; only the details surrounding Gacé's suicide were slightly edited.

"I couldn't let him go, Nanda," he said flatly, "not after he had read that memorandum."

"I know, darling," she said quickly. "I'm not blaming you."

"I've sent for Gacé's steward and for the local priest," Stanford said, holding her hands so tightly they hurt. "I shall tell him Gacé was shot in an accident and that we want him buried next to his former wife."

"They will investigate," she whispered. "There will be questions."

"We won't be here to answer them," he returned grimly. "I want you to put together a few changes of clothes for yourself and for the children. Your dresser, Miss Fergus, and Miss Braxton will have to come as well. Tell them to get ready. We are leaving at dawn."

She stared at him. "But Matthieu! We can't just go and leave him."

He looked into her horrified eyes and spoke reasonably. "Listen to me, Nanda. There is nothing you can do for him now. Our staying here to see him buried would only result in placing us all, including the children, in danger. He has friends and relatives in Baden. They will bury Gacé, and in consecrated ground, which they would not do if they knew the truth about his death. For our own safety, we must leave Niederwald immediately."

There was a brief silence as Nanda collected herself.

"You are right, of course," she said finally. "I will give the orders to pack."

"Good girl," he said approvingly as she rose to her feet and went toward the door.

Once there she turned to him again. "How many carriages are you planning to take, Adam?"

"We will have to take two. I can't risk leaving those women behind. They might all end up in prison if I do."

A thoughtful frown crossed her brow. "We could take one if you drove and I rode beside you."

For the first time that day Stanford smiled. "You are a woman in a million, my love," he told her with absolute sincerity. "We will take one carriage."

She gave him the ghost of an answering smile, nodded, and left the room with her usual, swift grace. Stanford went back downstairs to see that Gacé's body had been put in the drawing room and to talk to the steward.

They were on the road at five the next morning. Nanda had awakened the children herself and, when they were dressed, had brought them into her bedroom for a brief talk. They had sat quietly listening to her explanations, and the only sign of distress they gave was that Ginny had reached out to take Marc's hand.

"Adam brought Papa's body back last night," she concluded her carefully created tale gently. "He says it is dangerous for us to remain here at Niederwald, as the French agent who shot Papa will set the government against us all. Father Wellerstein will see Papa is buried next to Ginny's mother, and when the war is over we can come back to see his grave, if you want to do that."

Marc's eyes were enormous as he asked hesitantly, "Is Papa here in the house now?"

"Yes, darling. Do you want to see him?"

Marc and Ginny looked at each other, then they both shook their heads.

"All right," Nanda replied steadily, "that is up to you." She walked to her window and looked out. "The carriage is ready. Let's go."

The memory of that headlong flight through Germany was to remain a nightmare memory of Nanda's for years to come. It was over three hundred miles from Niederwald to Stade, and Stanford drove it in two days. They stopped each night at about nine and were on the road again at dawn. During the day they stopped only to change horses, which took little time as Stanford had made arrangements for fresh horses on his initial journey from Stade. They ate while the horses were being changed.

By the time they reached Stade they were all exhausted. Stanford, who had done all the driving, looked the least tired of them all. There was an old wood-hauling boat that had been in the harbor for repairs for a week, and at three in the morning Stanford boarded his party. They sailed on the morning tide.

The disreputable boat was commanded by Lieutenant Edward Singleton of the Royal Navy. He apologized to Nanda for the lack of luxury on board. "Lord Menteith told us we might have to wait awhile for you," he explained, "and we thought it best not to attract too much attention. The Stade channel is full of boats like this."

Nanda had told him sincerely that any place that could offer her a bed and a wash looked like heaven, and since the *Bremen* could offer both those amenities, everyone with Stanford was satisfied.

The only awkwardness occurred when Lieutenant Singleton asked about Gacé. Following Stanford's orders, Menteith had given the navy to understand that Gacé and Stanford were engaged on a secret mission for the War Department, and might need rescue by the Royal Navy if their activities were discovered. So Lieutenant Singleton had expected to be rescuing the Duc de Gacé as well as Stanford and Gacé's wife and children and dependents.

When the young man had said, "But I say, where is the duc?" Nanda had turned and left the cabin, leaving Stanford to make whatever explanations he had thought necessary. When Lieutenant Singleton learned that Gacé had been shot and killed by a French agent he had been horrified. Nanda's beauty had made a great impression on him, and the thought that his own thoughtless words had been the cause of reviving the pain of her loss appalled him. He had said as much to Stanford, who recommended that he leave the apologies he obviously wanted to make unsaid. "The less that is said to her grace about her husband, the better," he advised, which statement was perfectly true, although not in the way Lieutenant Singleton had understood it.

The weather was beautiful, but there was very little wind, so the *Bremen* made slow progress as it went up the Elbe and out into the North Sea, this time to turn north toward the shores of Northumberland instead of south to Dover. The first day Nanda spent most of her time with the children, who clung to her company as the only stable thing in their rapidly changing world. Stanford helped as well. He had taken Marc and Ginny around the ship, and Lieutenant Singleton had allowed them both to hold the wheel for a time.

By the second day they were both rested and feeling much more like their old confident selves. One of the sailors had a pipe, which he played to Marc for hours on end. Another crew member, a wizened sailor of at least fifty, showed Ginny how to tie knots. At dinner that evening both children were full of chatter for the first time since they had left Niederwald.

"Where are we going, Mama?" Ginny asked curiously. "Back to London?"

"No, darling," Nanda answered composedly. "We are going to stay at Adam's home for a while—Dunstanburgh Castle in Northumberland."

Two pairs of surprised eyes stared at Stanford. "My father has invited you all for a visit," he explained easily. "He has heard all about you and wants to meet the children who have had as many adventures as you two have had recently."

They both looked very pleased with themselves. "Rescued by the Royal Navy in the nick of time," Ginny said, complacently.

"Napoleon couldn't catch us!" Marc chimed in boastfully.

They both sighed with satisfaction. A good night's sleep and two days of doting attention by their mother and every other adult on the boat had done much to restore their equilibrium. Nanda's eyes, warm with amusement and gratitude, met Stanford's.

He rose from the table. "Come on, you two," he said. "Bedtime. Let us find Miss Fergus and Miss Braxton." As Nanda made to rise he gave her a quelling look. "You stay there," he told her firmly. "I will escort these two young hellions to their respective caretakers and then come back. I want to talk to you."

Surprised, Nanda sat back down again and Stanford shepherded the children out the door.

He was back in fifteen minutes, to find her still sitting where he had left her. There was a look of faint amusement in the depths of her eyes. "Did they go?" she asked.

"They went," he returned, an answering gleam in the blue of his own gaze. "Come up on the deck for a little while, Nanda. I really must talk to you."

"Very well." She rose with smooth grace from her chair and walked to the cabin door. They went up the stairs and out onto the deck. The crew were up front and the women and children were below in the sleeping cabin. They were alone.

Stanford turned to look at her as she stood beside him at the railing. They had been alone together for hours on the box of the carriage, but he had needed all his energy and concentration for driving and consequently had paid little attention to her. They had both been so concerned with the necessities of flight and of reassuring the children that they had barely spoken to each other except on those two topics.

Now, for the first time since they had left England, they were truly alone. The sun had set and the moon was up, filling the deck with a white light that showed him her face almost as clearly as if it had been day.

She wore a serviceable brown cloak pulled over the plain russet-colored dress she had worn for the last two days. Her hair was severely pulled back and knotted securely in a chignon at her nape, a style that afforded him an excellent view of her profile as she stared out at the moonlit water.

Her nose was sunburned from the long hours spent on the open box, but otherwise the face was the same as the one that had haunted his dreams for months. She turned and regarded him gravely. "What do you want to say to me, Adam?" she asked in her rich, slightly husky voice.

For the last few weeks he had thought of her mainly as a responsibility, someone whose welfare he was strictly charged to guard. And, because of the weight of that responsibility, his feelings toward her had been detached. As she, wrapped up in her concern for the children, had been detached from him.

But now the sight of her in the moonlight, the sound of her voice, brought back the piercing desire which had always hit him like a blow whenever they had met previously. More than anything else in the world he wanted to reach out and pull her into his arms. He wanted to

possess her, now, this minute, right on the deck of this
ship.

But her own face held no answering desire, and he
knew he must not claim her, assert his rights over her as
a conqueror, or he might lose her altogether. So he
forced himself to turn away and stare out at the night,
hoping she had not read his feelings in his eyes.

"We must make some decisions about the future," he
began resolutely. "I arranged for us to go to Dunstanburgh because it has easy access to the sea and because
you can be quiet there. I can go up to London and deal
with any questions that might arise."

She looked at his set, stern profile. "You said Matthieu
made a will naming me as guardian of the children?"

"Yes. I have it with me. Menteith is the executor. I
shall turn it over to him."

"I see."

He turned to her abruptly. "It was the best way out,
Nanda. Gacé knew that."

"I know it too, Adam." Her voice was calm. "I have
been thinking about it for days now. There is no point
in either of us saddling ourselves with a useless burden of
guilt in this matter. What happened would have happened no matter what our personal relations had been.
The fault was Matthieu's. It is only right that he be the
one to bear the punishment. And we will do what we
can for him. His name will remain clear—which is what
he would have wanted most of all."

As he listened to her quiet voice he felt a deep sense of
thankfulness for her. She was so . . . so sane. He felt
suddenly very peaceful, as though her words had healed
an ugly wound he had refused to acknowledge even to
himself. For reasons that were purely personal he had
hated Gacé, and so, paradoxically, being the instrument
of his death had left him with an uneasy conscience. Listening now to Nanda's sensible voice, he knew that she

was right. There was no point in feeling guilty over
what had been inevitable.

He turned to her, and the lines of his mouth were suddenly very tender. "And what about us, my love? What
are we going to do?"

"What do you suggest?" she replied steadily.

"I suggest that we get married. Right away. At Dunstanburgh. Perhaps your mother would come down for
the ceremony."

Her great dark eyes told him nothing. "There would
be a great deal of talk," she said. "I do not mind it for
myself, but I do not want to hurt your career."

"There will be talk if we are married now or if we
wait six months, or more. It will die down eventually
and it won't hurt my career. If it were up to me, I
would marry you right now, on this ship. But it is not
just up to me." He tipped her face up so he could see it
clearly. "Do you want to wait, Nanda?" he inquired
gently.

Her face was pale in the white light of the moon, and
he did not see the sudden color that faintly stained her
cheeks. "We had better not delay too long if you want
your firstborn to be named Todd and not de Vaudobin,"
she said, her voice huskier than usual.

He looked like a man who had been suddenly hit over
the head. "What?" He stared at her in stunned amaze-
ment.

At his look she laughed shakenly. "Don't look so surprised, my love. What we have been doing for the last
few months would get anyone with child."

"Oh, Nanda." Wordlessly he reached out and pulled
her into his arms. "Why didn't you tell me before?" he
asked, his cheek against the smooth browness of her hair.

She closed her eyes and breathed in his scent, grateful
for the roughness of his coat under her cheek and the
strength of his arms around her. "I've only been sure for

the last few weeks. There was no sense in burdening you with a problem you could do nothing about."

He held her even closer. "This settles one problem, then. We'll be married immediately."

"Adam. What if people say you were responsible for Matthieu's death? If you marry me—"

"Stop it, Nanda." He held her away from him and looked down into her troubled eyes. "Menteith will protect me. He will say that he ordered the mission Gacé and I undertook. After all, it is highly feasible. Gacé had many acquaintances in Baden who were likely sources of information, and I am well known as an intelligence officer. No one will be able to prove that the story I shall tell is false. That is all that counts. If people want to whisper—let them. I don't care."

The absolute sincerity of his voice carried conviction. It was true, she thought, with a wild sense of relief. He didn't care. She smiled at him. "I love you," she said.

"And I love you," he answered. The flame of desire began to beat through him once again, but he knew he must wait. He wouldn't be able to stop at a kiss; once her mouth was under his he would want all of her. And not just once. The rest of their journey would become impossible. Better far to wait until they were married. It was the thought that he would soon have her to himself, and for always, that enabled him to step back now. Unsmiling, he regarded her. "Get some sleep, Nanda. In another day we will be at Dunstanburgh. Everything is going to be just fine."

There was a glitter in the blue of his eyes, and, seeing it, a tremor went through her. But she nodded slowly. "Yes. You are right. I will see you in the morning." She turned and, without a backward look, went to the stairs and walked steadily down until she was out of his sight.

Chapter 24

Thou art all the comfort
The gods will diet me with.

—*Cymbeline*, III, iv, 182-83

They arrived off Dunstanburgh one day later, as the sun was setting. Nanda, Ginny, and Marc looked from the deck of the ship up to the grim stone walls of the great medieval keep, and three pairs of eyes widened identically.

"My goodness, Adam," Nanda said faintly to Stanford, who was standing behind her. "I had no idea Dunstanburgh would be so formidable."

He grinned. "It belonged to John of Gaunt at one time, but its been in the Todd family for the last four hundred years. It is more livable than it looks on the outside, I assure you." Nanda, well acquainted with the discomforts of several Scottish castles she had visited, looked dubious, but said nothing.

Stanford directed the boat into Embleton Bay, where the Todd children had kept their own small boats moored for years and where there had been someone stationed to watch for them. In a short time Nanda, children, and servants were climbing down the rope ladder into small dinghies waiting to row them to the shore. By the time they had all landed two carriages had arrived from the castle along the private coast road to take them back to Dunstanburgh.

The castle as seen from the land was quite as awesome as their view of it had been from the water, but Nanda found the cannon-dented walls less frightening than the thought of meeting Adam's father.

Lord Dunstanburgh was waiting for them in the great hall. He was obviously greatly relieved to see his son. The blue-gray eyes he turned on Nanda were polite but aloof. He made no mention of the absent duc, but saw to it that his guests were escorted to their respective bed-chambers almost immediately. He was flawlessly courte-ous, but Nanda could sense his anxiety to have his son to himself, and she obligingly ushered the children and servants on their way as quickly as possible.

Stanford watched her disappear up the great staircase and then turned to his father. "Well, sir, I could use a glass of brandy. Shall we go to the library?"

"An excellent idea, Adam." Lord Dunstanburgh led the way, and when they were seated before the comfort-able fire, with glasses in their hands, he said simply, "Well?"

Stanford took a sip of the brandy and stretched his feet out in front of him. "It's good to be home," he said contentedly.

"It is good to have you home, but that is not what I meant."

The light from the fire glinted on Stanford's tanned face and amused smile. "I know what you meant, Papa. I am merely trying to collect my thoughts."

"I see," Lord Dunstanburgh said noncommittally, and the look of amusement on his son's face deepened.

"I think I'll begin from when I landed in Stade," Stan-ford said thoughtfully, and, staring into the fire, he proceeded to recount to his father the story of the last several weeks. He told the simple truth except for the immediate circumstances of Gacé's death. That section of his story he edited to agree with the version he had recounted to Nanda. His father, who had known that Stanford had no intention of returning with Gacé alive, was not deceived. But he said nothing.

"And that is all of it," Stanford concluded some half an hour later. "Nanda has agreed to an immediate wedding, and I should like to be married in the chapel here at Dunstanburgh. I thought perhaps we might send for Lady Menteith, Nanda's mother. If both you and she are present some of the gossip will be quieted."

"Nothing is going to quiet the gossip that will surround this marriage, my son," Lord Dunstanburgh said gruffly. "Wait for half a year, at least. If you marry her now, people will say you had something to do with Gacé's death."

Stanford shrugged. "That can't be helped, sir. Besides, I don't imagine my feelings for Nanda are a great secret. We may be accused of bad taste for rushing the wedding, but that is probably all. It won't bother us, I assure you."

"Won't her children find it a bit hard to accept, coming so soon on their father's death?" The earl's voice was dry.

"Possibly, but I doubt it." Stanford sounded indifferent.

"Dammit, Adam!" For the first time Lord Dunstanburgh's temper began to slip. "I am not asking you to give her up. Just to wait for a decent period of time."

"You don't understand, Papa." Stanford's voice was patient. "It is not possible to wait."

There was dead silence as the meaning of Stanford's words registered with Lord Dunstanburgh. The earl's face looked decidedly grim as he stared at his son, then Stanford raised his eyes, more startling than ever in his bronzed face. He smiled at the earl, and his face looked suddenly young and vulnerable. "I'm so happy, Papa," he said. "Be happy for me."

At the sight of that look something shattered inside the earl, like glass breaking. He had been deeply unhappy about Adam's wish to marry Nanda de Vaudobin; he had resented her quite bitterly. But now, as he looked

at the unshadowed joy on his son's habitually reserved
face, all his objections came crashing down.

If any doubts had lingered they disappeared when
Nanda came into the small saloon where the family usually gathered before dinner. Stanford and Lord Dunstanburgh had been chatting quietly in front of the Beauvais
tapestry when she appeared in the doorway. She greeted
them both in her lovely low-pitched voice, and the earl
saw her exchange a brief glance with his son. It seemed
to him that an invisible current had leaped between
them, and from the way the rigidity had gone out of her
back Lord Dunstanburgh knew that reassurance had
been sought and given. If they could communicate like
that with just a look, the earl thought, then there was
nothing more anyone could decently say.

The next day Lord Dunstanburgh sent someone to
carry a letter from Nanda to her mother. They could
not reasonably expect to see the Dowager Lady Menteith for at least six days, and so they all settled down to
pass the time until she arrived. Stanford spent most of his
time in the library, where he worked on an official report for Menteith and Lord Bathurst; a private letter to
Menteith had gone to London with Lieutenant Singleton.
Stanford also was engaged in drawing up a proposal of
his own to submit to the foreign secretary, Lord Castlereagh.

Stanford wanted to organize an intelligence department which would set up and monitor a network of
agents who would be scattered throughout Europe. The
kind of information most useful to governments did not
get passed along through diplomatic channels, as Stanford well knew. It was not learned at embassies, but from
the gossip of ballrooms, bedrooms, sports parlors, and social clubs. Information was often as valuable as gunpow-
der to a nation engaged in war. And once the war was

over, a nation's whole future course of action could depend on the accuracy of its judgment about past enemies and allies.

Stanford's part in the Peninsula war was over, but the taste of life at the Horse Guards had whetted his appetite. He wanted to run an espionage department, and he had little doubt that he could convince the government that it needed one.

Nanda had been full of encouragement when he mentioned the idea to her. She was so relieved that he was not going back to the Peninsula that she would have applauded almost any other plan he put forth. She left him scrupulously alone while he toiled at the big desk in the library and spent her time with Lord Dunstanburgh and the children.

She was soon on comfortable terms with the earl. He, somewhat to his own surprise, found himself coming to like her very much. She was so unself-conscious of herself and of her beauty. Lord Dunstanburgh remembered several times the words Adam had used to describe her: "She has the kind of courage that not only gives but gives up."

The more time he spent in Nanda's company, the more Lord Dunstanburgh understood Adam's words. Before her husband had died she and Adam had been lovers, but no one who knew Nanda would ever make the mistake of thinking her a light woman. She was a woman for whom others mattered more than she did herself; a woman whose soft, gracious manners could not conceal an inner core of integrity and stability as strong as a rock. His son had not just fallen in love with a beautiful face. And she loved Adam deeply, of that Lord Dunstanburgh was sure. One had only to look at her face whenever his name was mentioned to know that.

And apparently her children loved him too. Far from being distressed about their mother's hasty marriage, they had been patently delighted. Lord Dunstanburgh found himself remembering back to the time when the twins were young and Adam had been a lofty Etonian. He had always been endlessly patient with his little brothers; teaching them to fish, to boat, and to swim during the long summer holidays. The twins had adored him, and it was obvious that Marc and Virginie adored him too. He was a man who genuinely liked children.

Lord Dunstanburgh was a man who liked children also. After they had been in residence three days, Marc and Ginny were calling him Grandpapa. And Virginie, in particular, had him firmly wrapped around her very pretty little finger.

Nanda watched her with Lord Dunstanburgh, a look of amused tenderness in her eyes. "Your father positively dotes on her," she reported to Stanford.

He laughed. "You must remember that my father never had a little girl, just great noisy boys. She makes a fuss over him and he loves it."

"He is spoiling them both to death. And when my mother gets here, it will be worse."

"It won't hurt them," he said calmly. "In fact, I think we ought to leave them in the charge of their adoring grandparents and take a honeymoon. Just the two of us. Alone. Together. For once."

They were standing together in the window of the library, which looked out over the sea. The sun was shining brightly and drew glints of blue from his neatly brushed hair. She took a deep, happy breath. "I would love that."

He turned and smiled down at her, and there was the deep silence of peace in the sun-filled room. They loved each other and in a few days they would be married. For now they were content to wait.

Lady Menteith arrived a day earlier than anyone had expected. From her manner one would have assumed she was summoned to hasty weddings every day of the week. She charmed Lord Dunstanburgh immediately. She also made him feel a great deal better about their children's marriage. No one would dare to question a contract sealed in the presence of the elegant, sophisticated and utterly delightful Dowager Lady Menteith, he reflected with a good deal of relief. He understood perfectly why Adam had sent for her.

She stood on tiptoe to kiss Stanford. "I'm delighted to be getting such a good-looking young man into my family," she told him. "The Dounces have a reputation to uphold, you know."

He laughed, as he was meant to, and the awkwardness he had expected to feel in meeting her again never materialized.

She asked no questions. One shrewd look at her daughter had told her all she needed to know about the reason for this quick marriage. She had seen that iridescent, glowing skin on Nanda once before. And if that had not decided her to acquiesce in a wedding that was unquestionably food for gossip, the shine of happiness in Nanda's eyes would have. Lady Menteith truly loved her daughter and had suffered bitter pangs of guilt over Nanda's marriage to Gacé. It was a marriage she had promoted, making one of her rare errors in character judgment when she had decided Gacé could make her daughter happy. The look she saw on Nanda's face now made her heart rejoice.

They were married two mornings after Lady Menteith's arrival, in the chapel of Dunstanburgh Castle. Nanda wore a shell-pink morning dress and no jewelry except the ring Stanford had given her a few days earlier. It had belonged to his mother, and now the diamonds flashed in the sunbeam from the high window as she held out her hand for him to put a plain gold band on it.

They spoke their vows in quiet, assured voices, and

when the ceremony was over turned to greet their family with the gravity of people whose joy is too deep for the ordinary business of smiles or laughter. Even Marc and Virginie seemed impressed by the solemnity of the occasion and were more subdued than usual.

They left for Lord Dunstanburgh's lodge in the Cheviot Hills immediately after a sumptuous wedding breakfast. As Stanford got into the carriage beside her, Nanda gave him the first smile he had seen from her all morning. He took her hand and held it tightly. "I feel young," she told him. "I haven't felt young in years."

He pulled her into the hollow of his shoulder, his arm around her, his cheek on her sweet-smelling hair. His own face was vivid with youth. "I know exactly what you mean, my darling." He kissed the top of her head lightly. "But we are neither of us exactly decrepit, and I trust we still have a few good years left." He grinned. "I can't believe I've got you to myself for two whole weeks. Do you have the stamina for it?"

Her rich laugh rang out. "What do you think?"

His eyes narrowed and he kissed her, quick and hard, then put her resolutely away. "If you continue to sit in such proximity, Lady Stanford, I won't be able to wait in order to find out. I suggest we occupy our journey in a manner that will take our minds off—other things."

Amusement and tenderness still lurked in the curves of her mouth, but she replied solemnly enough, "We could always count sheep. That occupies Marc for hours."

Their eyes met briefly, and a spark seemed to leap between them. They turned resolutely to their respective windows. "One," began Stanford doggedly, "two . . ."

Concluding Note

On July 21, 1813, the English army under the Duke of Wellington decisively defeated the French, led by Napoleon Bonaparte's brother, King Joseph. The battle was one of the greatest strategic triumphs in British history. It was received by loud public rejoicing both in England and in Europe. In London the prince regent gave a grand fête at Vauxhall Gardens for a crowd of 8,500 people. In St. Petersburg for the first time in history a *Te Deum* was sung for the victory of a foreign army. In Vienna Beethoven composed a symphony in honor of the Battle of Vitoria. Most important of all, the alliance of Prussia, Russia, and Sweden against France was joined by Austria. The end of the war was in sight: at last Europe was united against Napoleon Bonaparte.

ABOUT THE AUTHOR

JOAN WOLF is a native of New York City who presently resides in Milford, Connecticut, with her husband and two young children. She taught high school English in New York for nine years and took up writing when she retired to rear a family. THE COUNTERFEIT MARRIAGE, her first book, is also available in a Signet edition.